quare fellas
new Irish gay writing

Edited by Brian Finnegan

Basement Press
DUBLIN

Copyright © individual authors 1994
Introduction © Brian Finnegan 1994

All rights reserved. Except for brief passages quoted in newspaper, magazine, radio or television reviews, no part of this book may be reproduced in any form or by any means, electronic or mechanical, including photocopying or recording, or by any information storage and retrieval systems without prior permission from the Publishers.

First published in Ireland in 1994 by
Basement Press
an imprint of Attic Press Ltd
4 Upper Mount Street
Dublin 2

A catalogue record for this title is available from the British Library

ISBN 1 85594 100 7

The moral right of individual authors has been asserted.

Cover Design: Brian Finnegan
Origination: Verbatim Typesetting and Design
Printing: Guernsey Press Co. Ltd

This book is published with the financial assistance of The Arts Council/An Chomhairle Ealaíon, Ireland.

Contents

Introduction	5
Nataí Bocht *Eamon Somers*	13
Graffiti *Keith Ridgway*	29
Quare Man M'Da *Michael Wynne*	43
A Spoonful of Sugar *J J Plunkett*	53
Kit *Gerry Scott*	63
Hindered in the Interval *Anthony Newsome*	71
Watling Street Bridge *Keith Ridgway*	79
Near the Bone *Cherry Smyth*	93
The Inheritance *Jo Hughes*	101
Raindancing *Anthony McGrath*	113
Waiting for the Girls *J J Plunkett*	121
Tallaght Trash: The Diary of a Drag Queen *Attracta Cox*	131

INTRODUCTION

> 'What is straight? A line can be straight, or a street, but the human heart, oh no, it's curved like a road through the mountains'
> Tennessee Williams, *A Streetcar Named Desire*, 1947

When I was a young teenager growing up in the west of Ireland, I had a serious addiction to the sprawling family sagas that were the bestsellers of the day. It was in one of these tomes that I found my first literary mention of homosexuality; however, Patrick, the gay character in Susan Howatch's *Cashelmara* – a novel set in Galway against the backdrop of the Famine – turned out to be the most weak-willed character of the book while his lover was an inherently evil villain. Undeterred by this less than positive image, I went in search of more fiction that could give me a basis for self-identification. The next two books I read were found during a school trip to Dublin, tucked away in a corner of Easons – *The Front Runner* by Patricia Nell Warren and Larry Kramer's *Faggots*. These two novels remain some of the most memorable fiction I have ever read, simply because they opened a whole new world to me and they let me know I was not alone.

'We read to know we are not alone' is CS Lewis's oft-repeated line in William Nicholson's play *Shadowlands*, and nowhere does this apply more than to the gay reader. In Ireland, a country that is just beginning its journey out of the murky depths where state law is dominated by the ethos of the Catholic Church, reading has been an invaluable source

Introduction

of information and comfort for gay men and lesbians for decades. It is unfortunate that up until today much of this writing has been imported and that little of what we have read has reflected Irish gay experience in any way. There has been a greater wealth of writing for and by lesbians, such as Mary Dorcey's *Kindlings* or Linda Cullen's *The Kiss*, but gay men have been seriously under-represented. There have been many Irish gay writers who wrote about heterosexual experience, or who made veiled gay references within that framework. The homosexual subtext of Forrest Reid's *The Garden God*, published in 1905, caused consternation among gay writers such as Henry James. Brendan Behan, one of Ireland's most respected writers, covertly alluded to his own sexuality in much of his writing: *The Hostage* went on to become the inspiration for the transsexual element of Neil Jordan's film *The Crying Game*. Similarly, Irish gay men could often find references to their sexuality in the work of straight writers, for example James Joyce's story 'An Encounter', Brinsley McNamara's *The Valley of the Squinting Windows* and John McGahern's *The Dark*.

What makes the Irish gay experience different from other gay experiences? Until 23 June 1993 gay sex between consenting adults was illegal in Ireland. This, along with the Catholic line which says it is OK to be gay as long as you don't have gay sex, drove urban Irish gay men and lesbians underground and left those in rural communities with no room for difference and self-expression. The legacy of self-loathing and hatred which this systematic oppression has left with the Irish people has been very difficult to overcome, but its roots lie in another form of systematic persecution that lasted over eight hundred years. The Irish were once seen as the most trusting and innocent people in the world, but our history has made us very frightened. In our fear, the Irish turned to God for guidance, and put their trust in the Catholic Church. It is only because the Church has been so integrated in the development of Irish identity that the laws on homosexuality were not repealed until 1993. Ireland has always struggled to belong to the prosperous West, yet we have lagged behind in the revision of laws concerning morality, laws that will align us with our peers. Fear has been the key to our belated changes – fear of change and fear of disobedience.

Over the years, however, there has been in Irish society a certain hidden acceptance of homosexuality – most commonly an indulgence for eccentricity. Two of Ireland's most famous thespians, Micheál MacLiammóir and Hilton Edwards, lived quite openly together for almost fifty years and were not only accepted but quite literally revered by the Irish public. MacLiammóir's monologue in *The Importance of Being Oscar* – based on that other quintessentially Irish gay man – was seen all over the country and was greatly loved by the most ordinary of people, who were often moved to tears by his rendition of 'The Ballad of Reading Gaol'. The question is whether they would have found the same approval had they not been part of the theatrical world – gay men have always found the arts a stepping-stone towards fitting in with society at large. The histories of ordinary Irish people will show, however, that in rural communities there have always been gay men and lesbians who have fitted in and been silently accepted, albeit in heterosexual terms. It's probably the Irish propensity for sweeping problems under the carpet that allowed this to happen: because of our colonisation we have learned to look at ourselves through other people's eyes, and it is human nature to smooth over our inconsistencies for other people. The difference between other Church-driven countries and Ireland, in terms of homosexuality, has been the difference between active persecution of gay men and lesbians, and oppression through the simple denial of their existence.

When the Irish government finally did get around to decriminalising homosexuality, five years after David Norris won his case in the European Court of Human Justice, they

Introduction

went all the way. It was with joy that Irish gay men and lesbians greeted the news that not only were we legal, we were also granted a common age of consent with heterosexuals. In the short time since the passing of the Act, the sense of joy and freedom that has grown within the gay community has been palpable, and several other Acts have been updated to consolidate equal rights, including the Unfair Dismissals Act, the Medical Insurance Act, the Equal Status Act, and the Code of Conduct in the Irish army. Ireland is now seen in Europe as a leader in equal-rights reform, and we have been applauded for our bravery in the international gay press. Gay and lesbian groups are springing up nationwide and Irish gay men and lesbians are at last finding the courage to stand up and be proud of themselves for who they are. We are visible now, and heterosexuals are slowly beginning to understand that they have nothing to fear.

In general the reaction of the media, apart from the usual homophobic rantings of the tabloid press, have been positive and supportive. When I first approached Basement Press about doing this anthology, my proposal was that the book would begin to fill the gap in Irish gay literature, reflecting the feelings and experience of Irish gay men and lesbians in this time of optimism and change. Basement went one better and decided to do both a lesbian and a gay anthology. This led to the establishment of Ireland's first-ever gay list, Queer Views. My hopes for this list are high: there is a wealth of lesbian and gay talent in Ireland, and I believe that we have much to tell the world about our lives and loves.

There has been much talk of late about how gay men and lesbians have begun to ghettoise themselves, particularly at a time when we are being integrated with heterosexuals, at least in the area of marketing. Now that we are beginning to gain some power in the world, it would seem that on many other levels we are turning away from heterosexuals and saying that we are special in some way. The word 'queer' has been adopted in recent years as a non-gender-specific and political term to encompass all lesbians and gay men. Some see 'queer' as an angry and separatist term, but its real relevance goes back to its original meaning: 'queer' means different from the norm or usual, in a way described as odd or strange. To me the Queer Views books will be a series of different and unusual approaches to the norm, and as such will inform and educate people of all persuasions, and help with the integration of lesbians and gay men into the 'normal' fabric of Irish society. We may have an equal age of consent, we may be in search of equal treatment, but in so doing we have to be aware that equality is equality and in an ideal world, where everybody is treated equally, there is little or no room for separatism and ghettoisation. We must all, whether gay or straight, learn to live and let live.

It was not surprising to me that many of the stories submitted for *Quare Fellas* were about cottaging. This is a strong tradition in Ireland: for years, and even now, cottages were often the only guaranteed sexual outlet for gay men in rural areas and small towns to meet other men. The two cottaging stories I chose reflect this reality in very different ways. Eamon Somers's tragi-comic tale of tearoom manners, *Nataí Bocht*, tells of the mixture of misery and tenderness found in a public toilet in Galway, and of the need to battle the homophobia that has displaced us into this twilight world. Keith Ridgway's *Graffiti* bleakly witnesses transient encounters in a Dublin city loo, and the dangers that come with the territory.

The other stories here talk of times past, present – pessimistic and optimistic, fusing together as a whole to give an accurate picture of how Irish gay men live and have lived. Relationships with parents are poignantly portrayed in both Anthony McGrath's *Raindancing* and *Quare Man M'Da* by Michael Wynne. The latter is a multi-layered portrayal of love, desire, secrets and history from a writer whose

Introduction

rhythmical and structured language shows great potential. JJ Plunkett's *A Spoonful of Sugar* and *Waiting for the Girls* lightheartedly pursue the concerns of a young, carefree generation who have ditched the shackles of shame and guilt to experience life, sexuality and love for what they're worth, while Anthony Newsome's bitter-sweet *Hindered in the Interval* reflects on the feelings of an ageing drag queen quietly dying from AIDS.

Ever since Edmund White's novel *A Boy's Own Story* was first published in 1983, the definition of 'gay writing' has become blurred. White's semi-autobiographical book was the first gay novel to be hyped to a mainstream audience by a major publishing house; before this gay books were published by gay houses for gay readers. Now major publishers all over the world publish gay and lesbian literature: in 1994 Alan Hollinghurst's *The Folding Star*, an explicitly gay book, was shortlisted for the Booker Prize. If there is a blurring of the market for gay writers, there has also been a blurring of the ideas of just who can write gay fiction. Editors David Leavitt and Mark Mitchell, both gay writers, chose to include work by women and straight men in their anthology The *Penguin Book of Gay Short Stories*, and Leavitt's definition of the gay story as 'one that illuminates the experience of love between men, explores the nature of homosexual identity, or investigates the kinds of relationships gay men have with each other, with their friends and families' has been here adapted and set in an Irish context. Under this interpretation the sexuality or gender of the writer is immaterial, and although most of the writers in *Quare Fellas* are gay men, I make no apologies for the inclusion of two stories by women. Cherry Smith's *Near the Bone* and Jo Hughes's *The Inheritance* are both seen through the eyes of returned emigrants, a situation pertinent to most gay men in Ireland. Many of us are returned emigrants – we left a country where we were not able to become ourselves and we have returned in the knowledge that we can now be accepted and valued in law and in life.

It is becoming clear that many gay men have chosen to return to Ireland since the changes in the law were implemented, and it is likely that many more are coming to a decision to do so. I am a returned emigrant myself and there was a time when I thought that I would never be able to lead a happy life in Ireland. It is not the changes in the law that are bringing these people home; it is the result of the changes in the law. Unlike Britain, the Irish authorities found it mostly pointless to enforce their laws against homosexuality. But although mostly unenforced, the legal status of gay men and lesbians was a major contribution to our invisibility and our silence. Under Irish law, if we spoke out about anything to do with our sexuality, we spoke about something that was illegal. Since all this has changed Irish lesbians and gay men have become visible in the world, and Ireland has become known as a progressive country. The thriving gay lifestyles we lead, and have led underground until now, are there for all to see. Gay men are therefore seeing that it is more than possible to lead a normal, healthy and happy life, without compromising their sexuality, in Ireland. They are being given an option denied them before, an option that most Irish emigrants hold close to their hearts: the option to come home.

When I did return to Ireland the first thing I noticed was a startling integration of gay men and lesbians into Dublin's straight scene. Because of the size of the city and its gay scene, but also because of the easygoing tolerance of many straight people of my generation, I was able to go to straight pubs in the city centre with my boyfriend and physically express my affection for him. But the most wonderful thing I experience during my first summer home, just after the law reform, was the Pride march in Galway. Marching through the narrow streets, I was shocked and delighted to see people of all ages, male and female, smiling and waving as we walked past. It was a

Introduction

startling indication of how far Ireland has come in such a short time, of how open our people have always had the potential to be – and it gave me an optimism I would never have believed possible when I left Ireland just seven years before.

Brian Finnegan
October 1994

Nataí Bocht

Eamon Somers

EAMON SOMERS
Eamon Somers is a 43-year-old sex kitten living in London with his bimbo boyfriend. Both enjoy a totally superficial existence, coupled with a penchant for nylon housecoats and fluffy slippers. Eamon has published several short stories, is looking for a publishers for his first novel, and is writing a second.

Trade-wise it had been a pretty miserable week. Rain had come continuously and seemed heaviest at those times of the day when it would have been reasonable for an American tourist or even a farmer's son, in the city shopping for the day, to have tried to escape from the group activities to seek out a little excitement and relief in Eyre Square.

May had been unexpectedly good with several conferences taking advantage of the Tourist Board's hotels promotion and we had a continuous stream of men using our facilities.

But now June had arrived and with it, unusually early dark nights and biting winds and continuous rain. The inadequately dressed and the natural grey of the square took on the pall of November. Even the flowers and trees looked surprised as if they also had been misled by the holiday brochures.

I was on duty alone when he came in. He could have been an English-born lad staying with his granny or a local or a country boy escaped from the family while they did something for which he wasn't needed. He looked cold. His head was bowed and his arms seemed to be pushing his hand through his pockets into his stomach to warm them. He had on one of those windcheater things that were just beginning to be popular in Galway that year although foreign tourists had been seen in them for years.

The hood was up and tied tightly about his face. He was wet right through and the nylon was sticking to his back and shoulders. His grey slacks and Dunnes Stores-type lime-green and black sneakers showed he had not been sheltering from the rain.

Now of course my motives were not entirely pure, but I did feel for him, looking pathetic and broken like a proud little sailing boat being towed back across the bay after getting caught in a sudden squall – the occupants green faced and quiet, retching no more.

He headed towards the end cubicle, which we always keep open just in case a tourist would not be familiar with Irish money. He pushed the door open and went inside. He slid the bolt behind him and that was the only sound from the cubicle for the two hours that he spent there.

I had been washing my hands and I finished off and waited a few minutes to make sure he hadn't come in just to see the commercial facilities. The new mirror installed by the Council for the start of the tourist season was already broken, so I couldn't inspect myself. But I checked my hair as best I could with my hand and looked down my front for any obvious turn-offs.

There's a routine involved in checking out visitors to make sure that they aren't there just for a crap. It starts off with checking under the door to see their feet position relative to the door and the pot. It gets more complex as the dance to eventual engagement is embarked upon step by step. Of course with beginners it's not easy because they expect you to take the lead and teach them the steps and enjoy yourself and keep an ear of concentration on the space outside the cubicle. Even then they may get frightened and rush off or get violent and beat you up.

However this one responded to nothing. Not humming, nor whistling, nor standing in front of the door, nor my coughs, my eye to the spyhole, my note under the door or anything.

If I was to go on I needed a name for him. In the old days before we made contact with our lesbian sisters I might have called him Orphan Annie because he looked so miserable, but the name that came into my head just then was Nat, the pathetic creature created by Louisa May Alcott. But it was too short for my tongue and I Irished it to Nataí Bocht (Poor Little Nat) in deference to my Connemara roots.

I entered the cubicle beside his, using my last 2p, vowing to myself to go home after this one last try and have a night in front of the TV. I tried the peephole but he was sitting there his head in his hands, his hands inches from his knees.

I stood up on the bowl and looked over the dividing wall. It was the very definition of supplication, of innocence; an image to be exploited or protected. It could be managed boldly from outside, assuming his desires, accepting the responsibility of knowledge of already-being-thereness, and relieving him of guilt for his first experience. Or it could be guarded, swaddled, cocooned, until miraculously, nurtured by non-stimulation he emerged ready to spontaneously pursue his desires?

'Are you all right?' I whispered, leaning my head over the wall. 'Would you like me to come over?' I was ready to climb down into his cubicle in spite of knowing that my ungainly nervous descent would put off all but the most eager trade.

But he sat there as if I hadn't spoken. He didn't move, nor show in any way that he had even heard me.

Is he, I wondered, even now, frightened, but begging me to come over or is he so far away he can't even hear me?

I wondered if he might be deaf, but I had to accept he was not ready for communication. My note was still on the wet floor, untouched, where I had pushed it under the door.

I stood back from the wall and tried to make myself comfortable standing on the bowl, my back arched forward because of the cistern, watching the entrance for any shadow that would indicate someone was coming.

I started whispering little comforts to try and get through to Nataí Bocht.

'It's all right,' and, 'we've all gone through it,' and 'In a few weeks you'll wonder what you were worried about.' And more things like these, but spaced out with silences until a half-hour had passed. The cistern felt like it was advancing towards me and getting bigger and bigger and my back – long used to stretching to unusual shapes – insisting there was no pleasure to be had from this pain, forced me to get down and rest.

I took up Nataí Bocht's position on my bowl, my head cradled in my hands, encouraging the pain to go away. I was just wondering if physical position inspired certain kinds of thoughts, and if imitating his position would facilitate communication, when I heard his door open and bang shut.

My first thought, I must admit, was that I hadn't another 2p and that he could at least have left the door open, as he had found it; some regulars expect an unlocked cubicle. But then I opened my door and watched him slouch out, cold and miserable and I felt a pang of guilt. I considered following him, but a touring American complete with very heavy rucksack entered and looked as if he would need help to get it off. So I stayed.

I share the toilet with several men who come in regularly offering and seeking and some of these came back the next day when the weather had improved a little. At least I had someone to talk to even if my services were not required. Not that we were really in competition with each other, it averages out over a season. It's a bit different with some of the queens who breeze in on a Saturday afternoon or evening, looking as if they had never been in a public toilet in their life and looking contemptuously at us who should have been thanked, for keeping the place going all day, every day, in shifts, to make sure no one would go away totally disappointed.

The weeklies, as we called them, expected us to stand back and allow them have any pretty boy or fresh tourist that came in, as if it was their right to pick and choose. But this was only Tuesday, so those of us on duty stood around having a giggle; waiting, but enjoying ourselves anyway. I told them about Nataí Bocht, although I mentioned no names and said he told me to fuck off, just so they wouldn't think I hadn't been pushy enough.

Mairtín, from out Speidil way and a bit hard in his attitudes, got into an argument with Liam, who is from the city and a bit likely to make light of everything no matter what feelings or taboos are involved. Both of them were happy to give me advice but I wanted none of it.

'Well,' I said, 'I doubt if we'll ever see him again. But if we do I'll stand well back and let ye both have free rein.'

Not that that shut Mairtín or Liam up. They kept it going on and on and when they got fed up baiting each other, they turned on me. They dragged up my past failures one after another until Mairtín mentioned the Swedish lad, doing a course at the university, I had wooed one summer.

'You worked so hard; you tried everything; every approach you know and I stood beside him and he practically pushed me into the cubicle, his flies undone and his tongue hanging out.'

I'd had enough and I made an excuse and started to leave. But I was only halfway to the door when who walked in only Nataí Bocht, looking exactly the same as the day before: clothes, face, posture. Except of course he wasn't wet. His eyes paid no attention to me, but were lowered, watching the floor, wet and covered in dirty papers, in spite of the let-up in the rain and the Council's daily clean.

'Hello,' I said not expecting anything more than a small acknowledgement of yesterday's adventure. But I might as well have been addressing the sea up at Blackrock for all the attention I got. He headed for the end cubicle, just as he had the day before, pushed the door in and closed it behind him.

I executed a bow, removing my imaginary plumed hat with a graceful flourish at Mairtín and Liam, and said, 'He's all yours, darlings.'

Part of me wanted to stay and watch their humiliation, but if either of them succeeded the rest of me wanted to be walking round the Square when it happened. So I left and, walking against the one-way system, watched the cars filled with smug workers, mostly male, on their way home.

No doubt one or two watched me, my jeans worn to excite, my eyes not afraid to stare long after they had looked away a second time. But all I felt for any of them was contempt. I could see them at home ruling with instructions, loving with directions, displaying affection with cautions, squashing the unknown with fear and bribery; recriminations, warnings and threats.

Out of what awful, decent home was Nataí Bocht trying to find love? In spite of what anger was he willing to wait for the unknown? What hatreds would he have to overcome before he would even glimpse happiness? Just one more eighteen-year-old trying to find love on his knees, on the dirty smelly urine-soaked floor of a public toilet.

I went round the square twice before I ventured back. There was quite a bit of satisfaction for me in the fact that neither Mairtín or Liam had induced a better response from Nataí Bocht than I had. And yet I was angry that he couldn't see any of the three of us as fellow flesh and blood. I was angry that he didn't instinctively respond to one of us. Whether it was love he wanted or sex or some sort of confirmation that he wasn't alone – Mairtín or Liam or myself would be as good a first experience as he was likely to get.

I wanted to shake him and tell him that virginity was no binding guarantee of love, no Santa Claus present to be delicately unwrapped. It's a strangulating, limiting shell of hard grey stone that like the rock on the fields of Connemara has to be smashed and removed before there's a chance of anything growing.

He should be begging for someone to remove it, to liberate him, not guarding it like it was his one chance to buy some sort of unattainable, all absorbing surrender. What was in store for him only some lonely self-hating soul filled with an equally desperate passivity? 'Make it go away,' I could hear them both silently scream, hating each other for being liars.

I glowered at Mairtín and Liam and they giggled and mouthed 'PMT' to each other. I went to the second cubicle and stood guard over Nataí as I had done the previous day.

Nataí Bocht

More than a week passed with Nataí Bocht coming in every evening, going straight to the end cubicle and occupying it, without reference to anything outside, for two hours. During that time many men, old and young, good-looking and plain, came and tried that door with as much success as a communist running for president of the USA.

His two hours were spent sitting on the pot, his head in his hands, his face a few inches from his knees. For all the movement, or awareness he showed of his surroundings, he could just as easily have been at the men's sodality, listening to a visiting Redemptorist describing the fires and pains of hell.

For most of his two hours I stood on the pan in the next cubicle watching over him, wondering when his agony would end. I got down from my perch when my back ached so much I thought of the cistern behind me as a malevolent machine sending out icy stabs of control-removing pain. Sometimes I had to get down to drive away very pushy types. Men driven wild by the helpless victim they saw through the peephole and thinking they could unload all their own dammed-up imprisoned love onto this young man who'd had enough smothering generosity lavished on him already. They insisted and insisted again that he must respond, must surrender.

Mairtín and Liam and many regulars made comments which just showed they did not understand what we were both going through. It also showed that somehow they had forgotten their own first experiences. Of course we did remove two cubicles from service at the busiest time of the day and without giving any satisfaction to anyone. One or two of my own regulars were surprised that I appeared unavailable and unmoved by advances that had been successful in the past; making them doubt the sincerity of my previous responses. Others thought I was in my mid-life crisis, standing up on the pan, my back pressed against the wall like some cartoon mouse, frightened, hysterical.

And then it happened. I was down from my perch, trying to get some feeling back into my upper spine and missed it. When I resumed my position everything was different. Nataí Bocht was in the arms of a man. Nothing was happening, in the sense that I witnessed no movement, no gory details, no crying or sighing. They were like old friends from Eastern Europe with arms locking their vulnerable fronts to each other, excluding all others. I wanted to go and chase everyone else out of the toilet and to stand guard outside until they were ready to come out. But it was Saturday evening and the facilities were busy with tourists from abroad and from Dublin coupling with mountainy and bog queens from Connemara and Mayo and as far north as Ballina.

There was a desperation as well as a sense of fun and business about the place and more than enough to go round; so they were unlikely to be disturbed. I vacated my cubicle and it was immediately occupied by two men, smiling to cover their embarrassment and fear as well as their excitement at the thought of what they were about to do. I washed my hands, humming and letting the water gush noisily so that whatever went on in the end cubicle would remain private for Nataí Bocht and his partner. I wished them a joyous and fulfilling time.

Nataí's first experience would have to remain with him for ever so it should be as easy as possible. It was good that it should be over soon, finished, except as a pleasant memory. Subsequent experiences would merge into a natural satisfying way of life to be taken for granted like sunshine in summer or sleep in tiredness.

I walked up and down along by the urinals like an expectant father at an old-fashioned birth waiting on news. In the end I went outside on to the Square and merged with the evening strollers taking the mild mid-summer air. A busload of American tourists were just going into dinner, raincoats on or carried over arms, although the only walking they would do would be from the bus to the restaurant and back again. But if they weren't obliged to take coats with them everywhere, what would they talk about when they got back home? Of course I couldn't help wondering who was with Nataí. What was so special about him? Was just the moment that was right? Somehow after eighteen or nineteen years of denial and two full weeks sitting on the pot, he had known the time was then and the man he was now with had pushed an unlocked door, little realising how much had changed, how time had been right for him and not for many others.

But I only had to wait to find out who he was. I had already noticed the red wavy hair, the slight bald patch, the rather loud red bomber jacket and blue jeans. A well-built man, a little younger than myself but not so much. I puzzled over who he might be, if I knew him, if we'd been intimate at some time. I hoped we had and that I'd treated him well. I almost couldn't wait and I had to talk myself out of rushing back into the toilet and peeping through the spy hole.

It turned into a weekly affair after that. Nataí came in on a Saturday evening and only stayed until just after his partner had left. I knew Peadar of course. I had been one of his early conquests, but he only ever visited the Square on Saturdays. He was from Baal, a tiny village stretched along a street so wide that people hardly dared cross it without an overnight bag. He was an auctioneer's assistant when I met him, but no doubt he had progressed since then.

If Nataí's instinct had said 'Open the door to this man,' then it was as right as it could be. Peadar was generous, but without the desperation of many. He was known to buy meals and drink, to bring his lovers for a drive and if any had a mind to, to accompany him on his frequent trips to Dublin. He could chat and smile with a young man he had just met as if he had known him all his life. He was ideally suited to first experiences because he was decisive and assured without being aggressive or demanding. He could sense what a man wanted and chat reassuringly, bringing out a response that even in the imagination would have surprised his partner.

When they were in their cubicle I hovered outside or kept guard in the adjacent one. I often wonder what exactly they did, but it was only on the last occasion I saw Nataí, that I actually stood back up on the pan and peeped over the wall.

It was a gloriously sunny Saturday evening with a great busy buzz in the Square for the long August weekend. Everyone in the city seemed to be determined to enjoy the release brought about by the vast improvement in the weather. I'd been at a party the night before out on the Clifden Road, full of older professional men and any stray young things they could round up. I didn't really fit in so I drank a bit too much to prove I did and woke up very late that day. When I arrived on duty in the Square it was already late afternoon and I was surprised to see Nataí lounging outside on some concrete blocks assembled for repairs to the women's toilet.

I knew it was a sign that he was ready to move on in some way and my feelings of pleasure for him churned with regrets that my part in his life was finished.

There was no doubt he had changed. He looked, well, just more proud, more at ease with himself. His shoulders were held back and his head was up, looking at the world, insisting he had a place. His clothes were no different, although he had the windcheater thing off and tucked into its purse and strapped round his waist. His hair was more blond from the sun and as I went in to the toilet I watched him comb his fingers through it slowly and look across the Square to where Peadar was walking towards him, as if anticipating the intimacy to come.

I sat on the pan in the second cubicle, heard them come in and waited for several minutes before trying a view through the peephole. Although not papered over, I could see nothing. Silently I stood up on the pan and closed my eyes,

Nataí Bocht

waiting for my breath, made short and noisy by the thought of what I might see, to return to long and silent. Outside I could hear people using the range of facilities and beyond that the excited buzz of the tourists trying to prove they were really on holiday.

I opened my eyes, lifted my head and leaned nearer to the dividing wall. They were standing just inside the door clasping each other in a rigid, charged embrace. They appeared paralysed by their own intensity and oh, such energy I could feel from them that my breath once more became short and noisy. I ducked down for fear they would hear me but smiled knowing that they could hear nothing but each other's breath and noisy joy and moan at having survived another week of anticipating and aloneness.

Even I, so well practised in public sex that one ear is always radar-sweeping the surroundings, heard nothing until they were at the cubicle at the other side of me. There were three of them shouting – 'Come out you fucken queers' – and kicking the door and then throwing one of the concrete blocks that Nataí had so lately posed on over the door.

I crouched, waiting for my turn, checking the bolt was locked. They kicked and shouted and I knew to wait and press myself back against the cistern, my hands up-poised, and when it came over the door I silently, painfully, deflected the block away from me. I looked at my grazed palms and watched the blood come slowly, praying there would not be a second one, yet preferring another, to having my charges in the next cubicle disturbed.

But even as I leaned nearer to whisper something over the wall, the block arched over the door and down onto the pan; where Nataí had spent those first weeks, and smashed the porcelain.

Why did Peadar not know they would go away? Surely he knew they would kick the door and shout their abuse and then would get bored and go away? And me, looking over the wall and see his hand go for the bolt to open the door, why did I not shout to stop him?

He pulled the door closed after him as if to protect Nataí inside and I watched through their cubicle and over their door the tops of three heads facing Peadar and saw fists attached to wrists but little else aim at him without seeing the connections. And sometimes whole heads, with faces, on shoulders would appear high up over the top of the door and then come down noisily on where I imagined Peadar's face was.

Then all I could see was three heads looking down, but I could feel the kicks and then I looked in to see what Nataí was doing. It was as if my looking over the wall freed him from watching through the peephole in the door because he suddenly stepped back, tripping over a large chunk of the broken pan. He looked down at the china and picked it up.

And the door was opened again and his shoulders were stooped and his head was bowed just like the first time I saw him, except that instead of having his hands in his pockets, they were up in front of his face holding the chunk of pan, like it was the horns of a bull and he was playing a party game. Through the open door I could see one of the heads I had seen earlier and there was a body underneath it now and one of the feet was kicking Peadar lying on the ground and the head lifted and I could see the open white shirt and a tanned neck and then the blood as the sharp china pushed in and Nataí let his end go and the other's hands went up to take it and I thought how un-hygienic to handle a toilet bowl like that with blood everywhere.

The man staggered backwards, leaning into the urinal and seemed to slide down into it until he was sitting, his head to one side supported by the divider. The china and his clothes and the floor and even his hands, no longer holding the rim, all bright red from the blood spray. I had to look away and would have fainted had I not gotten down from my perch. Of course within seconds there were Gardaí and ambulances and onlookers and advisers. I came out as soon as I could and submitted to the attention, both soothing and menacing.

Peadar and I were taken to the same hospital. I was released after some hours but he was kept in for two weeks. The attacker went to the morgue and the chunk of toilet to the laboratory for fingerprinting. Nataí had run after he had pushed it deep into that tanned neck; run before the blood had sprayed on to him; run before the other two had time to stop him; run before anyone out on the Square realised anything had ever happened.

But I like to think that in that no-time between pushing and running, or even as he pushed, he looked down at Peadar and there was time for a feeling, an impulse of love, desperate or goodbye or impossible love, but something, before he was gone.

Over the two weeks Peadar was in hospital I visited him every day. I brought him fruit and cards and read out newspapers reports of the incident and reactive letters from several points of view. I asked him about Nataí, but he told me nothing, not even his real name.

Now we are a type of friends. We don't talk about him, but he keeps us together. The Gardaí never found him and I'm pretty sure Peadar hasn't seen him either. I still carry on my duties much as before. The Council has made some changes to the toilets, but we do our best. Peadar still comes down on Saturday evenings and seeing him makes me long for an ending. Is Nataí back home after his holidays or tending cattle as his people would have him or is he someplace waiting quietly, perhaps now and again thinking about us – kindly?

GRAFFITI

Keith Ridgway

KEITH RIDGWAY
Keith Ridgway was born and lives in Dublin. His poems have been published in the Sunday Tribune, Poetry Ireland Review, Salmon *and others. His short story 'On a Scale of One to Ten' appeared in the anthology* Hairy Tales, *published by Basement Press in 1994.*

1st Person

A pulse of something caught his eye, just a bright stab of something in the corner, like a face turned differently or a reflected button or the small sharp movement of a hand. It was not the man immediately next to him, nor the next one on. It was the third, he thought. He was afraid to raise his head to look, the wrong one would look back. He swivelled his eyes as far as he could without actually moving. This allowed him better to sense, not to see, the man, two down, the third one, the one who had done something, he was sure of it, that was directed at him.

His cock became a little harder in his hand, and a strange sensation clenched his jaw. He leaned forward a fraction, enough to cause the man beside him to turn his head and stare, adjusting his hand slightly to reveal more of his penis. He cursed the man silently.

He quickly put his cock away and zipped up and moved past the three men to the sink at the far end. As he passed the third man he looked at the back of his head, hoping he would turn. He didn't. He was in his late twenties, quite tall, well built. He wore bottle-green jeans.

The sink was filthy. He knew the hand-drier did not work so he placed only his fingertips under the running water, staring at them for a moment before looking up and to his left, back to the third man, now closest to him, to find himself looked at and almost immediately smiled at. The face was friendly and attractive.

The cubicles stood facing the sink and the long, undivided urinal. He made some show of trying to dry his hands and then turned and chose one, delving into a coat pocket full of pennies to open the door. He slipped inside and let the door rest against its lock but not close. He held his breath. After only a few seconds the door swung open and the man in the bottle-green jeans came in, still smiling. He let the door close fully behind him and turned the lock.

'Hi.'
'Hi.'
'What are you into?'
'I love to be sucked.'
'So do I.'

The man with the bottle-green jeans moved up against him and rubbed his crotch gently, finding his hard-on and gripping it through his trousers. They opened each other's belts and buttons and zips and caressed each other's cocks and balls. The man in the bottle-green jeans pushed his hand through the other man's legs to find his hole and to rub his buttocks. To do this he had to crouch slightly. Then he went down on to his knees and took the man's cock into his mouth, sucking it gently at first and then moving his head back and forth.

After a while they swapped positions and the man in the bottle-green jeans had his cock sucked. He groaned loudly, making the other man nervous, and the other man stopped and warned him.

'Oh, I don't fucking care.'

But that was the end of the sucking. They pulled each other off, managing to come at the same time. The man in the bottle-green jeans again groaned loudly and his come landed on the other man's sleeve. The other man wiped his penis quickly and pulled up his trousers.

'Thank you,' he said.
'Well, thank you.'

He went out of the cubicle, leaving the man in the bottle-green jeans alone.

2nd Person

There was a sudden quiet as the door slammed shut. He pulled up his jeans and sat on the edge of the toilet seat with his eyes closed and his chin on his chest. After a while he took out a cigarette and lit it. When he had finished smoking he went out and washed his hands, drying them on a tissue.

Graffiti

The two men who had been there earlier had either left or gone into another cubicle. The urinal was empty now, except for one old man who stood with his head against the wall, yawning. He did not seem to notice that there was someone else there.

Out on the street he felt cold. It was nearly dark and he decided to get something to eat. He bought a newspaper and walked to a fast-food restaurant where he ordered a cheeseburger and chips. He read the paper and ate slowly. The front-page story was of a big storm on its way, coming over the Atlantic and swooping down on the country, taking cold from the north. There would be gale-force winds, perhaps hurricane force, and there would be torrential rain. Structural damage was expected – broken windows, falling slates.

When he had finished eating he smoked a cigarette, reading the TV page and the horoscopes and the cartoons. Then he looked around for the toilets. The gents consisted of a single urinal, one cubicle, and a sink. He went into the cubicle and put toilet paper all around the seat before sitting down. He looked at the graffiti, being sure to check the door jamb and the sides of the toilet-paper dispenser, and craning his neck to see behind him. Most of it was bad jokes and names and initials. At eye level to his right was written:

For gay sex here 6pm

There was no date given. Further down on the same side was:

I love big dicks

and underneath someone had scrawled:

Fucking faggots.

He took out a felt-tip pen and drew a picture on the back of the door.

Outside on the street he could not feel any wind, and there was no sign of rain. He stood for a while at the corner and looked at the sky and looked around. He could sense people's expectation of a storm, but not the storm itself.

There were few cars around and fewer people. They hurried along purposefully, checking their watches and looking out for buses. He saw a man in a business suit stop a taxi. A little further down the street two women with a suitcase watched, annoyed, as the taxi passed them. They followed it with dirty looks. They were there first.

He walked down towards the river, not really paying too much attention to where he was going, for the moment at least. He wanted to walk off his meal a little before going back to the public toilets. He decided he would turn down the quays to where the rent boys usually hung around. He just wanted to have a look, perhaps make some eye contact.

There were only two there that he could see, both leaning against the river wall, facing the street. He slowed his walk down to a stroll as he approached the first of them, a young man in his early twenties with very short hair and a thin moustache. He wore a track-suit top and jeans and was smoking. Their eyes met, briefly.

The second one was younger, about sixteen or seventeen. He had shoulder-length dark hair and wore a full track-suit. He was quite pretty and smiled easily.

'Ya wouldn't have a cigarette, would ya?' he asked.

'Yeah.'

'Thanks very much.'

He lit it for him and their hands touched.

'That's great, thanks. I was dying. Bleedin' freezin' isn't it?'

'It is a bit, yeah.'

'Are you doin' business then?'

'What do you do?'

'Anythin' ya want basically, y'know, fifteen quid.' He paused for a reaction. When he didn't get one he added:

'Ya can fuck me for twenty-five. With a condom, like.'

'Where?'

'Have you got a place?'

'No, I don't.'

'Well, we can go to the toilets then.'
'No, it's too dangerous.'
The boy looked at him and smiled gently.
'Sure it's added excitement,' he said.
They both laughed quietly.
'Isn't that what it's all about?'
'It probably is. I'll leave it for tonight. I'll see you around.'
'Alright. Would you have any odds at all?'

He gave him five pounds because he liked him, and they parted with smiles and a friendly wave, each thinking himself a little richer.

He continued on and crossed the next bridge, turning to walk up the way he had come, but on the opposite side of the river. They were building here, huge cranes looming up out of the dark. He looked at them and wondered if they would be all right in the storm. He tried to work out whether, if they fell, they would be tall enough to bridge the river. He thought they probably would. Squash a rent boy. He looked across the water just in time to see his friend get into a car. He waited to see if the car would come around his way, but it disappeared down the river, heading towards the sea, making him feel foolish.

He stood there and watched the lights sparkling on the surface of the water, stretching the shapes of the city into bleary and strange cartoons. It was comfortable to look at and he did not move for a long time. He stood there with his hands in his pockets and felt himself relax. Some dull sensation drained away from him and left him feeling wide awake and strong inside.

There were even fewer people on the streets now, and he puzzled this over as he made his way towards the toilets. There was no wind, he could see no clouds. He could see stars, though not many, and he could see a sliver of pale moon hovering high above the streets. It was a beautiful evening. He supposed that everybody was staying at home, checking their windows. It didn't leave him feeling very optimistic about the toilets, but he knew he had to go and check them anyway. He had little choice.

Two policemen stood at the corner. They were looking up at the sky. One of them glanced at him as he passed but he knew there was no need to worry. They did not really care, and he turned back towards them before going into the toilets, to see them looking upwards again, their hands in their pockets, their caps tilted back.

The toilets were empty. All the cubicles read 'Vacant' and he sighed as he stood at the urinal, expecting nothing, and annoyed that nothing would happen. The feeling of excitement was missing, the blend of fear, disgust, shame, pleasure. The potential. The electricity. It was the ritual that drew him here, the sense that he was a figure in an age-old dance, unconscious of the steps, sure-footed. He took part and moved on. He hadn't started it.

He considered what to do. He could go home.

He zipped up and walked along the row of cubicles, gently pushing each door. They were all closed. When he reached the last one he put in a penny and went inside.

It was remarkably clean, and very spacious. He had often wondered why there was so much room. Perhaps whoever had designed them had understood that they would have more than one use. He liked that idea.

The walls and the back of the door were covered in small neat graffiti. Most of it was simple one-line requests, followed by a series of dates and messages. *('You weren't here.' 'Missed you, make new date.' 'How will I know you?')* There were some large blocks of writing which described real or imagined experiences in great detail. He enjoyed reading these to spot the deliberate spelling mistakes and disguised handwriting. He recognised some of the drawings as his own. One in the centre of the door had almost faded away, so he took out his pen and went over it. All of the other drawings were crude and childish in comparison to his. He was the only one who put in faces.

He sat on the toilet seat and lit a cigarette, reading the walls for anything new. But there was never anything new, there was only the same thing written differently. Some people wrote their ages, but they lied. According to these walls nobody was over thirty. Most of the time there was nobody there under thirty. But there was a different kind of time there, maybe they became confused. It was self-contained. Nothing on the outside touched them, nothing in their lives felt close to them – it seemed a fiction.

He took out his pen again, trying to think of something to draw, smoking his cigarette and tapping his foot. He yawned and his eyes watered, a sudden simple weariness coming over him. He wanted to go home. Leaning down with his head between his knees he reached out to the very bottom of the wall with his pen. He wrote:

Did you ever think you'd sink this low?

He sat back and looked at it. It was small enough to force you to lean down, but big enough to catch the eye. It was a small act of subversion and he was pleased with it, pleased with the halt it would cause. But he knew it would not be stronger than the ritual.

He threw his cigarette into the toilet bowl and flushed.

Outside the cubicle he raised his head to see a man standing at the urinal, looking at him. Well, well. He went to the sink to wash his hands. He had not heard the man come in and he was surprised and interested. The man was a little older, perhaps thirty or so. He had a shuffling, nervous look, as if this was relatively new to him, as if he had also thought that he was on his own, as if he had also just decided to go home. He was tall and thin, with wispy hair and glasses.

They looked at each other.

The man in the bottle-green jeans went into a cubicle and left the door open. After a moment the man in the glasses followed him. They did not speak. They moved against each other and kissed, and their hands worked with buttons and belts. Almost immediately the man in the bottle-green jeans dropped to his knees and took the other man's penis in his mouth. It was limp. He concentrated on making it hard.

3rd Person
The man in the glasses leaned his head back against the wall and closed his eyes and felt the soft, wet warmth envelop his cock. He felt the other man's hands move up over his stomach to his chest, caressing him. His cock became hard as the man moved his head back and forth and moved his hands down again to feel his balls and his ass. He opened his eyes and looked down. He saw the man's head moving, and his own cock going in and out of the man's mouth. He saw the man's wrist against his balls, his hand hidden between his legs. It was only then that he saw the man's other hand come out of the pocket of his own trousers, lying in a heap around his ankles. The man in the bottle-green jeans was stealing his money.

'Hey!' he gasped, pulling away.

The man in the bottle-green jeans stood up quickly and went for the door, trying to close his belt with one hand as he moved. The man in the glasses was pulling up his trousers, raising his voice.

'Give me my money. Give me my fucking money.'

He buttoned his trousers and stuck out a foot to stop the door swinging closed. Outside the cubicle he grabbed at the other man, who swung around and pushed him.

'Give me back my fucking money.'

'Fuck off.'

The man in the glasses felt a panic and an anger surge through him, stronger than he was able to contain. It spewed from his mouth.

'You cunt, you fucking cunt. Give me my fucking money! You stole my money!'

The man in the bottle-green jeans seemed to step back, to hold his breath at the force of this. It was the noise, the volume – it seemed to scare him.

'Shut up,' he hissed, quiet and quick.

It gave the man in the glasses a certain sense of having the upper hand. His panic eased a little and he was sufficiently aware to conceive of a tactic. There was a small silence between them, staring at each other, poised differently, differently balanced, one moment in which they considered themselves, as though detached, as though it was all theoretical. For a moment, they were not really there.

Then the man in the bottle-green jeans shuddered, as if suddenly disgusted. His whole body gave a little involuntary shake, and he closed his eyes for a second. Then he looked at the man in the glasses with an intensity that he seemed to have discovered inside himself. It was strange enough, unexpected enough, to send the man in the glasses back a pace, to frighten him into thinking about what it was exactly that he was involved in here. His route to the back door was closed off to him. The man looked stronger than him. Did he have a knife? He looked like he might have a knife. Which pocket would it be in, left or right? Should he make a run for it now, forget the money? Go which side? Left or right?

Without warning, the man in the bottle-green jeans swung on his heel and started towards the door. The man in the glasses felt his anger surge back through him. There was no knife. He lunged forward, letting out a cry as he did so:

'You're not going fucking anywhere!'

The two policemen walked through the door, bumping into the man in the bottle-green jeans, with the man in the glasses at his back.

'Okay, what's going on?'

Everything stopped. He was sweating just a little now. He knew he was in the right so he did not rush in with his explanation. He took his time, collected himself, breathed in, breathed out. He was okay now, the police had arrived. They would look after it. He just had to tell them that he'd his money stolen, his pocket picked.

Then everything started again. The man in the bottle-green jeans didn't even look at him, he just started talking.

'This faggot tried to fucking rape me. You can't come into one of these places without some pervert drooling all over you. Look at him. Look at him.'

They looked at him.

'I don't believe this. He's lying.' He said it quietly.

'Fuck you,' said the man in the bottle-green jeans, cutting him off, 'you should be locked up.'

'Okay, okay, take it easy please. Did you try to interfere with this man?'

'He stole my money.'

'Oh, fuck off. He came at me with his dick hanging out. I push him away and he starts screaming at me – you heard him.'

'Do you want to make a complaint against him?'

'I want to go home. Can you not just beat him up or something?'

Both the policemen smiled.

The man in the glasses did not understand what was happening to him. He felt himself shaking a little, the sweat running down the back of his neck so that he had to wipe it with his hand.

'Why don't you go home now, please, sir?' one of the policemen said to him.

'I don't believe this. He's got my money. He stole my money.'

'You're claiming that this man has stolen your money.'

'Yes.'

'How?'

'He picked my pocket.'

The two policemen looked at each other.

'How did he manage that, sir?'

He paused. He knew that they saw it.

'While I was standing here.' He motioned to the urinal.

'That's ridiculous. He's making that up.'

'How much money have you lost, sir?'
'About thirty quid. And I didn't lose it.'
'Would you empty your pockets, please.
'You want me to empty my pockets?'
'Yes, please.'
'But he's the one who stole...'
'We'll get to him in a minute, sir.'

The man in the glasses dug into the pockets of his trousers and pulled out some coins and a handkerchief, and then turned his pockets inside out.

'Okay?'
'And your jacket.'

He replaced the coins and the handkerchief and then took some keys, a glasses case and another handkerchief from the pockets of his jacket.

'Okay?'
'Okay. Now you, please, sir.'

The man in the bottle-green jeans went through the same procedure. From his jeans he took some coins, a single five-pound note, an empty packet of chewing gum and a crumpled tissue. In his jacket there were keys, cigarettes, a lighter, a blue felt-tipped pen and a rolled-up newspaper.

'Satisfied?'

The policeman turned to the man in the glasses.

'It was more than a fiver you said you'd lost, wasn't it, sir?'

'Yes. He has it on him somewhere. I don't know...'

The policeman took him by the arm and led him down towards the sink. He leaned towards him in a conspiratorial way, but his voice came through clenched teeth.

'Well, sir. I don't see any evidence here that you've had any money stolen. Now if you insist that you have had money stolen by this man then we'll call up a van to take you both down to the station, where this man will again be given a chance to make a complaint against you concerning a sexual assault on him. Now unless you're pretty sure about what you're doing, I suggest you cut your losses and fuck off home before I loose my temper.'

He kept his face very close. His breath smelled of cigarettes and plastic. The smell of a chewed pen, the smell of glue. They looked at each other.

'Okay?'

'Okay.'

'Good.'

They walked back to the other policeman and the man in the bottle-green jeans.

'Let's all go home now please, sir, this gentleman is willing to forget about his money. Okay?'

The man in the bottle-green jeans shook his head and sighed. Then he stared at the man in the glasses, turned slowly and left.

'You going to go home now, sir?'

He closed his jacket and walked past them on to the street. He was glad now just to be out of there. He did not look up.

It was cold. There was a wind starting. He could hear it whistle around corners, and he could hear the rattling it caused in the metal shutters and the signs. He made his way to his car without looking up. Then he sat in the driver's seat for a long time with his head resting on the steering wheel, not moving, trying hard to erase pictures and words from his mind. He could not. The noise he heard growing louder and louder, surrounding him, hammering at him, was, he realised after a while, the rain falling on the roof of the car. It ran down the windscreen in the continual transparent wash, like bleach.

Eventually he started the engine and drove away.

QUARE MAN M'DA

Michael Wynne

MICHAEL WYNNE
Michael Wynne was born in Sligo in 1971, and began writing creatively at an early age. In 1990 he brought out a short collection of short prose called Speak of Angels, *and his work has appeared in a number of anthologies. He is about to embark on a novel.*

Like a mother, proud, he mouthed the swollen lids, probed them with bunched, circled lips, felt the hooded mounds tremble with the pressure. Unclad, he slid outside the single cover, superimposed himself along the lithe, sheeted sleeper, breathed: Éibhear, it's Sunday, Éibhear, Éibhear.'

Propping pale arms, full-length, on each side of the prone motionless shape, soft groins pressing through thin linen, he dipped his neck, drew the point of his tongue the length of the grainy trenched chin, across the closed mouth puckering in the meditation of slumber, precisely through the strait of the philtrum, straight without pause to the tip of the smooth broad-tipped nose.

'Yes Éibhear,' he said in response to a short snort-carrying stir; again dipped his head to nip the side of the taut throat, nose-nuzzle the underchin, whispering calm urges.

Buttery sunlight tinting the wisps of his thigh, his buttocks, he chin-butted the other's chin, flipped his tongue along the underflaps of the warm moist lips. A shoulder rose, slipping from the sheet, which, tenderly, he nestlingly rested his armpit socket-like on while eyeing eyelids that, flinching and creasing, uncovered grey eyes, prominent, dream-dazed.

'Are you going, Conall, heading now?' Éibhear mumbled, flexing his neck on the pillow.

'I've a bit, a bit of time,' said Conall lowly, rolling from him, stroking the sleep-slackened jowl.

Heavily, Éibhear turned from him, eyes again lapsing; Conall, hands clasped at his nape, went to the sun-filled window, his shrivelled sliver, the head silver-scaled, shivering at a draught. From the window he watched the bend of the stream beyond the green sloping bank; looked away, yawning, to the walls of the room, white-washed, monastically bare; then back at the ripples and wavelets of the wending current. 'The longest,' he murmured, eyes riveted on the river, the heel of his hand kneading the root of his pudenda, pressing the crisp pubes – 'longest in Ireland'; and he laughed with slow depths across his shoulder toward the bed.

Éibhear, lifting his head from the cratered pillow a little, listened for what he'd missed, caught instead a steady inhalation, then a tentative restrained recitative –

'Oh the holly she bears a berry'

– with certain repeated bars rendered with a facetious formality. Parody, parodic, parodial. Declension. Very clear-headed, it's a wonder. His head sank back, languid eyes on the clutter covering the locker: sundry time-pieces; a phail of nitrate; tissue and foil scraps; Dylan's *Poems;* a supine gin-naggin, bone-dry. Dragging the sheet close so that it twined about his upper arms and thighs, he felt separate folds lodge in his posterior cleft, caress his underbody, form a firm sack around his scrotum. And Mary she bore

'...our Savior for to be,

And the first tree that's in the Greenwood...'

What did I dream of? The word 'tolly' stands out, all it entails. A goo-goo word, safe babbling baby slang speak. So-called protective nonsense term, substituting one thing with the same thing essentially. Pretty pointless, just results in having to re-learn. Any benefits? Tollywolly. Good to exercise formation of sounds. Who coined it?

Burying his head deeper in the pillow he breathed from the tick his, Éibhear's smell, and his, Conall's smell, emanations exhaled and exuded, intimate, mildly mucid, identical essences commingled.

And the tolly tightens, thickens, twitches towards tumescence. Am well awake now.

He stretched, loosening the sheet's embrace, low-hummed to Conall's continuing carolling, carried languidly with the climbing sun; then teased, 'Still singing the dirge – give it a rest, ride.'

Moniker from the outset, that. Sacrosanct handle. From

riding on the breadth of Eirinn for the ride, purely. Get a move on, ride.

From him he swished the sheet so it billowed a little, shifted his thighs so his arousal sprang from constraint. Argus-eyed he watched Conall approach: silently smiling, tight-lipped; hands hipped; sharp-pileated penis horizontal, a demanding flushed arrow. And at the same moment that Conall's shins rested against the bed-end, Éibhear switched position swiftly, like a lizard, so his head lay across the foot; stretching his neck, his arms out-splayed, he gazed directly upwards at the knitted dendritic gonads, the quivering levelled member.

'We have time?' he said, his fingers like tendrils reaching to the thighs. For consuming consummation.

'Yes, yes,' came the answer, restive.

Conall sank, sinking his face, his expectant maw onto Éibhear's fired, wiredrawn sex, his own likewise sinking into Éibhear's wet receptive mouth.

Connected, the swivelled to the middle of the expansive mattress, their penises sliding piston-like, smoothly synchronous, past slimy inner cheeks, lubricious palates, the ready entrances of seasoned gullets. Arms looped around each other's lower back, with heads undulating from side to side, mechanically impassioned, they took each other whole at each stroke, hands gripping, groping along tensed spinal trenches, furred buttocks and furrows: one fused, pulsing organism, the mutual consciousness sensually drenched. Simultaneously they felt the other tremor, surge and, surging, urgently quicken, then erupt, bolting curdled gobfuls of gobs which, unthinking, they swallowed like it was their own phlegm, nuzzling each other's softened hardness with soft porcine sighs.

As Conall slipped alongside him, Éibhear murmuringly kissed his shins, lapped the darkly filamented flesh, the broad bones, hands clamped in the constricted houghs. Did the oul' man do this in his day? In the mouths of men in our mouths: a clandestine oral tradition, tacitly carried, time out of mind. Hushed human music, mouth organed, rootsy. His earliest sentence, almost: the first remembered, said with pride as he searched my reaction for same: You're like me. How like?

Disengaged, he turned on his back, crossed his wrists at his abs, eyes loosely closing.

A little drained. Sex is arduous.

He felt the bed dip at his left, felt parted lips press on his eyebrows, his eyes, felt the flat of a tongue sweep his flank; Conall's words: 'I'll get ready downstairs and head off. Seeya love'; heard him leave, sonorously humming his hymn.

And the mousey as blood it is red. Playful terms for the dirty parts of the dirty body, dirty, dirty. The naiveté of common verbage, Dad fell for it of course. Some funny coinages of his, must have been his, the way he thought. What I dreamt of in part. Crack for fart, mousey, wolly, so on. And something else, my whole sonship encapsulated in a vision, seen from his eyes, his mind. Something very sexual in it. Looking down at his calloused hands, the veinal arms, that had become mine, mine through him, a dream-blent version of us, the arms and how- or hod-holding hands focused on because exposed mostly. And me in miniature centering him, not forgotten for a second, my child's mind concentrated on by him, a new universe expanding, requiring a clean flippant lingo. Like breaking into, raiding his brain. Was it like that?

He reached to squeeze the wispy testicles.

Wet drams induced by my father's suppressed potential, unrecognised otherness. Knowledge is impossible. Limits as it builds, reduces. Start out with all it takes, have our strengths whittled down as we advance. Delightful desires that make us gods if given free rein: nipped, lopped at from the word go. Pitiful.

Sleepily sitting, he lazily stroked his glans till the penis lifted from the pubis.

Quare Man M'Da

Begotten, not dead for ever. No necessity, however, for me to beget. Not now, no.

Delicately he worked his length with a ringed finger and thumb, a licked index searching beneath him for the fucked anus, the post-coitally tingling tract. Head lolling, his digit singing to the middle joint between the sappy walls, he held himself more securely, the palm facing outwards, and pumped himself with steady speed.

(Ah!) Dad's Aiden in civvies by the marriage bed throughout my childhood in Sooey with black greased hair in waves like slick liquorice who was he was never explained a dead friend killed in his prime Dad said a fine man seen as sexy then with oiled locks shoulders wide (ah!) a curved crotch distinct from the sepia tints like an icon on my mother's doilyed locker next to rosary-case psalter ribboned springs big mouth open a big smile a fine man all fine men back then (ah!) working the land till the backs nearly broke all red meat eaters Aiden his name was I knew it before mine a mystery man historyless with wide shoulders widelegged stance hands like scythes what a man bumped off in the prime of his prowess (ah!) writhing big-buttocked in my father's mind's eye through the build-up to my conception why not (oh!) shag a dead stud.

In two quick shots he cumlessly came, fetched deep-lunged breaths, his shoulders and neck flexed; rising at length from the bed he stalked across to a basin by the double-hung window, soaked his hands, pat-dampened his face and axillae, flicked glinting globules at his torso, his crotch. Over his shoulders to the furling Shannon he crooned,

'Woe betide you Shannon water
By night you are a gloomy river,
And over you I'll build a bridge,
That never more good sex may sever';

turned back to study thoroughly in the frameless facewide wall-mirror his dark gums, his tongue and quite even teeth, his hispid chin and jaws, the bleared bulging eyes.

Eyes dark-rimmed, fawny. You're like me, says he. Opening wide his mouth he peered in deep at the shiny pink-tinted uvula. Good night last night. First time for me to fuck at a club. Not for Conall. Something wonderfully primordial about it, hands gripping cold porcelain, the pubis and rump colliding, compressing against the other with the pall of piss around us, the fallen folds of denim at our ankles, all consciousness of self and nurture helplessly, sublimely abandoned with the wreathing, wrenching intenseness, privates on show to the sleazy strobe-streaked dimness, all holes bared with the heedless, happy hunger, shameless and helpless, the shared enormous hunger of us. Us. Concealed by nothing but the occasionally lasered dark, our moans merging with the muted thumping beat and the fervid thumping alongside us somewhere, the smell of men so fetid and heavy we could taste it nearly.

Reaching down he raised the lower window-sash to its extremity, directed a bright yellow jet, obliquely arced, so it plashed on slabs edging the embankment beneath. All last night's tipple drained off: pissed at the club, nips swiped as we drive, driving all night from the capital to Carrick, full of the hard stuff and stiff, stopping off for a feel outside Longford, to fondle our longs. How horny we were. And reckless. He brayed a laugh, his wrists crossed against the embrasure above him, his sun-gilded trunk leaning forward with the steam from his dick jerking to a dribble on the outer sill. Taste of him still lingering. Beautiful to see him again, in the exact same spot standing, shouldering the pillar, his foot on the step. Classy man he is, massive, as they have it, wherever they got it. Greeting each other with extended tongues, memories of the last westward trek rousing. Took no time to get back to. And remembered my name, Éibhear, Éibhear, so good to hear him freely use it, often. Introduced it at Mass perhaps, most ceremonious: If we may say a prayer folks, for Éibhear my fuck-chum. Renaissance is right. I'll dress.

From a chair by the bed he removed a pair of black jeans; a grey form-fit tee-shirt, a polyvinyl waistcoat, dark socks: he donned them in seconds and, stepping into crumpled boots, he left the room, descended a short flight to a cramped hall. In passing, he lifted from the newel post a faded green bomber jacket with an outline of Connacht cresting one breast, a red ribbon pinned awry to the other; smiling wryly, he dipped a finger in a Cross of Calvary font mounted by the light switch, lightly tipped the bridge of his nose, his lips, his breastbone. Stepping out of the house he carefully clicked the door after him and tuned down the bright street whistling, his thumbs looped. He entered a squat shop on the corner and bought a tabloid which he wedged into the jacket under his arm as he crossed the dusty deserted road to the church.

Antiquated shells, these, before long now. Anachronisms. Already hear of many turned into offices, secularised wholesale. And high time. Much more practical. Leave their outsides ornate, curiosities, bitter reminders to the last of the repressed.

Passing through a side-gate he passed, tensed, through to the shadowed, stout-pillared nave, through to a sombre chilly susurrating stillness. His view of the altar obstructed, he watched the leaning attentive bodies of the aged kneeling hearers. Very strange scene to me now. How I've grown out of. The embarrassing solemnity of.

He leaned forward likewise at the sound of the concelebrant's homily concluding, rhythmically paced, delivered in the resounding sonorous monotone of a divinity. Then wishing them a peaceful easy Easter Feast. And a 'Happy Easter, Father' from the drab-toned supplicants, dutiful, Godfearful.

Offer up the bloody body here. And as blood the willy's red. My childish pronouncements dreamed of, seems to suggest what we're fools to try sublimating: our carnality, its facets. Gas too, that hairy, weird episode, weird, Dad making a pass at me in his senility, me just out of the bath and he approaching, stroking my sternum, and the seminal smell of him, and pleasing. Why did you encourage me, Aiden, why, Aiden; and me wondering how far they went, how far, and how, and wondering how well did he once know how a man smells, tastes, how he sounds when in heat, and wondering how the hell had I ever suspected before I knew what there was or that there could be something to.

Sidling by the pillar he levelled his eyes on his fuck-chum, his Conall, high-collared and albed, standing commandingly, his person pressed to the altar-edge, holding the Host at arms-length above him.

And what do you do? I take striplings for Music and as I advise them on the crotchets I do cross-surveys on the crotches. And you? What do you do? And the land I had when he told me. You're what? Quare man m'Da. The Ulster expression, shows disbelief. Strange it is. But it's apt.

His hands pocketed, he watched on, waiting, thinking of imbibed inhibitions, inhibitions revealing dwelt on before being flagrantly, gloriously rescinded, before their hallowed, delicious relinquishment.

A Spoonful of Sugar

J J Plunkett

J J Plunkett
J J Plunkett is a pseudonym.

Everything Claire said sounded like it came from the script of a bad French movie. She had the habit of speaking in short sharp sentences, which she interjected into conversations at the most unexpected of times, and she always said the least expected things. With other people this may have become embarrassing, but with her it was always charming, both serious and amusing at the same time.

'He's fallen madly for you darling,' she once said, during a run-of-the-mill chat we were having about the antics of my latest boyfriend, a comment to which I could only reply with shocked laughter. We were sitting on the cobbles of Temple Bar outside The Norseman, drinking cool clear lager from plastic, pint-sized tumblers, on one of those beautiful afternoons in early September when the annoyingly unpredictable days of Dublin summer had evened out into the more constant airy warmth of early autumn. The city was not as awash with tourists and foreign students any more, so we were enjoying the relative lack of confusion in the air and the space that went with it.

'No,' I said. 'He isn't falling in love with me, he's just displaying his childish need to have everything in his life running smoothly all the time. Jonathan just can't handle relationships.'

Jonathan, the boyfriend in question, seemed to have disappeared from the face of the earth over a week before.

'Look at this beautiful thing,' said Claire, deftly changing the subject as was her habit. She held a small tubular keyring up to the light. It was filled with some kind of viscous clear liquid and when she shook it, tiny metallic stars swirled around inside, like those old paperweights we had at Christmas, in which snow danced around a plastic Santa and Rudolph. I had noticed it in the Zodiac shop we visited earlier and thought it looked cheap; now in Claire's delicate hand it seemed pretty and valuable.

'I stole it,' she said, 'I've been doing that a lot lately. Shoplifting, you know. I take things I don't need.' Whether I would have been shocked at this revelation normally, I don't know, shoplifting is not something I've ever contemplated. With Claire, the idea seemed to add to her charm, giving the objects she stole some kind of extra quality and value.

'It is beautiful,' I laughed, and she promised to get one for me next time.

Our paths had accidentally crossed only a month before this. We met while rummaging through a skip in Foxrock one August Monday evening. Skip-hopping is one of my favourite pastimes; my flat is completely furnished with the rubbish of the relatively wealthy, everything from the bright orange portable TV down to my cherished set of three chipped 'Alice in Wonderland' mugs has been found in skips outside houses in Foxrock or Howth or Killiney. On this particular excursion I was examining a tall, slightly cracked, blue glass vase when I heard a voice with a distinct Australian drawl saying, 'Can I have that?' I looked up to see Claire's small freckled face smiling quizzically at me from the other side of the skip. Giving her the vase without hesitation, I invited her back for coffee and since then we had rarely been apart. It was a small wonder my lover had disappeared; he must have been suffering from lack of attention.

Everything about her was a contradiction; although she was as tall as me, because of her precarious bone structure, she often appeared to be tiny. Her face was mouse-like, her hair fell around her neck in weak colourless wisps, yet in the way she moved her hands or walked, she appeared to be the epitome of style and sophistication. On the hottest summer days she was to be seen wearing a waist-length black jacket made out of wool, masquerading as fur. When it was cooler she would be half naked in tiny shorts and a hideous psychedelic halter top, which, of course, on her looked like Westwood or Gaultier. She always carried around a large overstuffed, brown leather bag, in which she rummaged endlessly but only ever produced a small engraved silver box and a plastic lighter. The silver box would be opened and Claire would roll thin mellow joints from Golden Virginia tobacco and grass which she claimed to have specially imported from Holland. Something in the way she repeatedly dipped into that bag reminded me of the scene in *Mary Poppins* when Julie Andrews produced the most unexpected objects from her own carpet bag. I almost expected Claire to tell me one day that she would only stay until the wind changed direction.

That day, as she examined the floating stars in her newly acquired keyring, I found myself, yet again, gazing unashamedly at her, admiring her beauty and trying to pin down its source. She wore a pair of hornrim-shaped, mother-of-pearl sunglasses and a black beret pulled clumsily over her ragged straggly hair. On her fingers were a large assortment of cheap plastic rings that clicked noisily on the tumbler from which she drank.

'You know we should really sleep together at least once,' she said, lighting one of her tiny joints. 'It would be fun.'

This change of direction in our conversation came as no surprise to me, rarely a day had passed, since we became close, that she didn't mention the possibility. I began to notice that she would raise the subject at times when I would be lost in momentary contemplation of her. At first the suggestion struck horror into my soul. What if I was unable to perform? Would she lose all respect for me?' But as time went on and I became more infatuated with her, more attracted to her incongruous beauty, the idea began to have a vague exciting effect. I would tingle slightly at the thought of making love to her angular body, at the thought of going that one step further with her. And so, on that autumn afternoon in Temple Bar, I found myself agreeing to the suggestion and eventually we began to plan the occasion with all the zeal of schoolgirls organising a pyjama party.

We decided to consummate the relationship at my flat. Claire lived in a crowded Harolds Cross squat where the other occupants roamed from room to room in a stoned haze, regardless of any need for privacy. In Marks & Spencers, on the day of the event, we bought two bottles of Chateau Chablis 1987 and a large tub of Haagen Dazs rum and raisin.

'The wine for before, the ice cream for after,' she called out, running to catch the number sixteen bus to work. I made my way home and began to tidy the debris of a month's neglect and laziness. In the living room, while picking up empty beer cans and emptying overloaded ashtrays, I quickly and almost furtively turned an abandoned canvas to face the wall, not wanting to acknowledge guilty feelings I had for neglecting my so-called 'calling'. My artistic endeavours had quickly taken second place to the sudden novelty of having Claire around; she seemed to swallow any inclinations I had for any activities other than sitting around, smoking and drinking coffee or beer.

These half-hearted efforts at cleaning, however, were almost immediately interrupted by a prolonged ringing of my doorbell. It could only be Jonathan, I thought, and sure enough when I opened the door there he was, six foot four and smiling pathetically behind a large bunch of gladioli.

'I brought these for you,' he said, thrusting the flowers along with a bottle of red Le Piat d'Or into my arms. 'I had to see you.'

'Well it's about time,' I replied curtly, turning around and leaving him to make his own way into the flat. I was more annoyed with him than I cared to admit. His disappearance, although unexplained, was tantamount to rejection in my limited book and I was suspicious about his feelings concerning my relationship with Claire. He may have been feeling neglected, but it was also apparent that he was caught up in his own attraction to her and resented the fact that she focused all of her attention on me.

A Spoonful of Sugar

'Treat 'em mean and keep 'em keen,' was the advice I got from too many friends, sick of my endless complaints about how he 'done me wrong', whoever He might have been at the time. I had been through a long string of meaningless relationships, in which I had misguidedly placed all the meaning I could muster. That's why I was so thrown by the next remark the neglected Jonathan made.

'I think I'm falling in love with you,' he said before breaking into a startling show of wet emotion, his head making a dive for my shoulder lest I visually witness the unmanly flow of real tears being shed on my account. Not knowing what else to do, I put my arms around him, still holding the wine and flowers, and hugged. So this is what happens if you treat 'em mean, I thought. What a learning experience life can be.

We drank the wine, smoked a few joints and made less than lucid love on my unmade futon. Jonathan explained, during all this, how he had spent the week wandering aimlessly around Galway trying to make sense of his feelings, spending his nights at a cheap Hotel in Salthill. It all sounded a bit too melodramatic for me, but who was I to complain? The attention made me glow with the light of one who is desired for reasons that go beyond the physical. After the sex, that light began to glow less and less brightly until finally I began to wish Jonathan would leave, and so I concocted some lie about having my recently bereaved aunt over to dinner, she needed someone to talk to and had chosen me, it was a pain, but I would call him tomorrow and arrange to meet at the weekend for a serious chat.

Claire phoned almost the moment Jonathan walked out the door.

'I'm leaving work in five minutes, I hope your ready for me!' she giggled down the line.

'Ready as I'll ever be.' My libido wasn't feeling very strong, but in the half an hour or so it would take her to get to my place I would have time to have a bath and change the sheets. I opened every window to relieve the air of the smell of sex that I felt sure was lingering in the room. During the few minutes I had to relax in the bath, I tried to turn myself on with thoughts of a naked Claire lying underneath me, our limbs intermingling in the best Hollywood style as we made hot celluloid love, but unfortunately there was no response in the groin department. I did find the idea attractive, but only in the most idealised way, an image I was sure would not correspond with the real thing.

Claire arrived while I was still in the bath, I jumped out, buzzed her in and rushed into the back bedroom to change into something more comfortable.

'Darling I'm home,' she called, walking into the room with a bottle of Moet and two glasses. 'I nicked these from the theatre for us,' she continued, ignoring my near naked, dripping-wet state. She tapped her green nail-varnished fingernails on the bottle, said something about deciding to be divinely decadent tonight in her best Liza Minnelli, and tottered off to the kitchen to put the bubbly in the freezer. I was too agitated to follow, the realisation that we were actually going to have sex suddenly froze me to the spot. Closing the door, I leaned against the wall and tried to tell myself that it was all a bit of experimental fun, that the outcome, whatever it was, didn't matter. Claire was my friend, everything would be OK. Smoke a joint, have a drink, calm down. As if to validate the need for casual indifference, I threw on a pair of old jogging shorts and an outsized t-shirt, lit a joint and made my entrance to the living room, where Claire sat on a fresh duvet, watching a re-run of *Dad's Army*.

'I never did get this,' she said making a gesture towards the TV and as I sat down beside her she suddenly, without warning, planted a large wet kiss on my lips. It was all over very quickly after that; we fumbled for a while with the condom, both in a rush to get the act over and done with, the final fulfilment of our appreciation for one and other. Her urgency surprised me and provided the stimulation to keep me going, as if her need for me created a belief in my own erotic powers with a woman, something I had no belief in myself. When we had finished I asked her if she had come, to which she replied, 'No, but it's alright, I had a good time.'

'I did too,' I said. 'Let's have that champagne.' And so the night went on, alcohol and joints and talk until dawn. Just as we were about to drop off to sleep she whispered in to my ear: 'Let's go to Amsterdamn when we get up.' I laughed lightly and said I'd think about it before falling into a deep slumber.

I dreamt that Claire was hanging on to the edge of a huge skyscraper, screaming at me to save her from the impending fall. When I gave her my hand to pull her to safety, her expression changed from one of panic to one of uncontrolled mirth; she grabbed my hand and pulled me down with her. I could hear her wild manic laughter as we both soared downwards towards the traffic-filled street.

When I woke up Claire had gone, it was easily four o'clock in the afternoon and my hangover was so great I just lay in bed for the next few hours going over the previous evening in my head, checking for embarrassing moments or revelations I may have made in my less than sober state. It has always been my habit, when drunk, to talk incessantly about myself, making stories out of things that aren't stories at all, the dull after-dinner speaker, immune to the boredom of others. Try as I might to correct this fault, alcohol always got the better of me and now as I began to realise how much I had monopolised the conversation, a peculiar kind of dread began to take hold of me, a fear, maybe, that I had indeed failed with Claire after all and that she had lost the respect for me that I so ardently craved.

As I dialled the number of her job at the theatre, a slight twinkling caught the corner of my eye and I noticed the keyring Claire had nicked in Temple Bar. Beside it, scrawled on the back of a supermarket receipt, was the note:

J J Plunkett

I still haven't found what I'm looking for.
Claire.

Her supervisor at the theatre wanted to speak to me and as I held on, waiting for him, I realised that I would probably never see her again. The note in all its minimalism seemed clear cut and final, the keyring a parting gift. The supervisor asked me questions as to her whereabouts. She had come in and cleared her locker out earlier that day and he was concerned about her absence.

This morning Jonathan brought me my breakfast in bed. 'She's finally made some contact,' he said, with more than a hint of hostility in his voice. There, leaning against the coffee pot, was a postcard of Sydney Opera House surrounded by sparkling Christmas lights. The postmark on the back, though, said Perth, WA, and on the left-hand side, written without a return address or phone number, was:

Paul, I have not forgotten you.
Love always, Claire.

KIT

Gerry Scott

GERRY SCOTT
Gerry Scott lives in Dublin. He studied art at college and has exhibited in Dublin and Cork. His visual work has appeared in various publications, and this is his first short story to be published.

> Squatting is not a crime. It can be a solution to housing problems. Increase your confidence in dealing with officialdom. Others can squat, so can you. Take control of your life.
> (*The Squatters Handbook*, 8th edition)

Woke to a white afternoon, what should have been a white morning. I'm lying here like some deposed head of state, lying here in a trance-like state, ceiling-watching. It's a popular pastime of mine. Actually I'm looking at the rectangle. The top half of the room is white, except for this one rectangle of orange, some remnant of a former tenant. The bottom half is a maddening swirl of deep green. Felt so disgusted with myself, waking up as late as I did and after all my wonderful plans. Plans gone out the window, out into the cold, sunny, snowy afternoon. It is true that I spend a lot of time in bed, but the paraffin heater needs fuel and those Chinese takeaway cartons had to come from somewhere. I emerge. A hand runs through a swab of greasy hair. No water hits my face again today. Eyes stay semi-glued together. These days I don't get to see my face as often as I would like. Just the occasional glimpse in a reflective shop window as I walk past. Caught one the other day. Don't worry, I thought, you still have it!

Now Brigette lives downstairs. I think I heard her rumbling about earlier. She was the one who told me about this place. That was when it was a possible basement in an open house on Tollington Road. That was when it was some words scratched out on a tatty piece of paper. Now it's a room on the ground floor, a hole in the window. Brigette has made a cosy little nest downstairs. I haven't really bothered up here. I won't be here that long. Yesterday I did clear up some, shifting other people's rubbish into the corner. These are things I find, maybe put them to good use some day. Those cinema curtains, I just found them, yards of unbearably itchy green fabric. All the bottles, candles, bags, all the stuff that in turn will become my rubbish. Yesterday, that was me making space in my room, room for Adam.

Brigette lives downstairs. I hear her outside my door, telling me the electricity is off and the water pipes are all frozen up. Brigette lives down there, dangerously close to the serial killer. In truth Chris isn't a serial killer at all, probably just a harmless child molester. Harmless. Loitering with harmless intent outside the railings of Stroud Green Primary. No, we don't know much, don't know anything about Chris. Just some crazed guy who we rarely see. It's easy to summon up a hideous vision. But the girl upstairs said the dog wouldn't go near him, or anything. Said the dog didn't sniff his crotch, and that cannot be good, she said. Dogs know.

So that's pretty much us: Brigette, Chris and the girl upstairs. Others come and go. Don't fool yourself, we're no family, nothing like that. And then there's me and Adam. And no, we're not lovers.

> Please remember, squatting groups are not alternative estate agents, dishing out rent-free accommodation. They can only help you to help yourself. They exist because people have come together to support each other and exchange information, skills and ideas.
> ('Finding a Place', *The Squatters Handbook*)

Well, you see they have these meetings all over the place. Our local is in Islington, Wednesdays. It's just the usual, the usual yacking away, setting the world's wrongs to right. All this together-in-community shit. All this while we stuff our faces. Toad-in-the-hole. That was the main reason I went along with B., I was starved. That was the night I met Adam. We were sat at table, Brigette and I, when he raised his head up from a bowl of the night's fare. Revealed a wet stew smile, topped off with a strawberry-blond flat-top. We got to talking. About what, well, I'm not sure. Later, Adam revealed that on that night I talked a lot. I'm rarely overwhelmed, so often under.

Adam is young, maybe my age, maybe younger. And he's quite beautiful. Well, that's what I thought. Stopped me in my tracks. He said he had just come out of the army. I didn't ask why. He didn't venture an answer. He comes from somewhere in Kent. I'd never heard of it. Anyway he's looking for a place, so I suggested our place. He's calling around tomorrow. For a look.

That night while ceiling-gazing I thought about this boy from Kent. And I thought that this could be my last night in this room, alone. And that felt good. That other than voices upstairs and down, there will be voices here in my room. Maybe laughter too. Adam's crackling Kent laugh. And all these thoughts zonk around in my head. Happy, I nod off into the land of same.

Tomorrow, it's here today. Adam is due soon, no point in me stirring out of my warm nest. Stay right here in bed. Or did I say I'd meet him at the underground or did he say that he knew the way? Later it will emerge that Adam knows the way most everywhere, prides himself on his sense of direction. Adam, a keen map-maker for those lost souls who don't know, or perhaps have lost their way. Adam is here. With him a large swag-bag, all his gear in it, all his kit. Kit, personal equipment especially packed for travelling, workman's outfit of tools, clothing for a particular activity or situation, a soldier's kit. Into the room, I'm all apologies for the paraffin stench. He says it doesn't matter, he says he likes the place. From his kit he produces a tape recorder and a pint of Unigate long-life milk. He says the tape recorder needs batteries. With him also, enthusiasm and a brightness, enough for two. And I felt some sort of silly warm glow in my room, in me.

When I came in he was sprawled out on the green cinema curtain reading an old *City Limits* magazine. The light is dim, light sponsored by Candles and Co. And that little camping stove that has been lit in the middle of the room. Kit scattered across the floor. Adam, happy in self-sufficiency, some sort of domestic bliss. Little blocks of fuel that spit and hiss and heat the soup, but not all the way through. Not fully warm, so we drink it lukewarm. Baxter's broth from enamel mugs, more army supplies. All his stuff is army gear, mostly coloured camouflage green, a means of disguise or evasion. I loose him in my room every night, lost in the green swirl. Looking at you and you caught me, and laughed. I laughed too, a nervous laugh, I guess. And we get to talking, rather you talk. I listen. But you know I really don't want to hear about your fucking girlfriends, and the fact you haven't got one. I have nothing to contribute to that conversation. The cars pass up and down Tollington Road; sometimes their lights shine in on us.

Euston, five minutes to nine, exactly. I know because I've just looked at the clock. Big, ugly, Seiko seconds click past. Four little nothing plastic seats, the ones that you gradually slip off. That's the idea. Four little yellow plastic seats, two occupied. Me and Adam, engaged. A very dirty little man approaches. He checks out one of the bins. Nothing. This creature, so fucking thin, is nearly blown away by the whoosh gush of an oncoming tube, destination Edgware. Now a mate of his appears. Travel in pairs, it's safer that way, I find. His mate asks me for twenty pence. I say that I'm as broke as he is. In his broad Irish accent he says that at least I can get out of here. Then he asks Adam for money. Then he asks everyone else along the platform. Later he joins up with his friend. Neither of them has found anything. Nothing.

On the steps of St Martin-in-the-Fields, just me. This is one of my favourite places. Everybody must have one, at least one, and this is mine. It rains lightly, orange drops of street lights dripping. It rains at the front of the church but here at the side I escape. But not from the wind which whirls through those wonderful grey granite columns. Some down-and-outs used to lie along these steps, all jumbled up together with blankets and coats, oblivious to the passer-by. No one here now, save me. I walk down a black shining street. Hair drips wet now on to my face. And nearby, in the lazy distance, I take shelter in the blue and pink neon interior of a bar. A bar whose name tells the truth, tells it like it is. Downstairs by the piano, by the columns, by the bar the people stand, boys and men. And a sprinkling of womenfolk too. Don't accept drinks off strangers – well, I guess that one won't hurt. A man tells me that he likes my hair. Then, he politely informs me that he likes me also. He is my reflection in the shop window for a day. A brief encounter.

In another bar, in Islington, they don't bother to ring any bells. And when the owner's wife, she's the woman in the white blouse, comes around collecting empties she doesn't shout in our ears that it's time either. In truth it was well after time, closing time. Even now there's a bleary-eyed woman holding on to the bar and shouting for another gin. No special reason why we're out, Adam and I, we just are. I think that we both vowed to come back again, but we never did.

Abstracts of time divide – well, they separated us anyhow. I remember when we got back into the house, but I don't recall the journey there. I suppose we took the number 19. When we got in it was bloody cold. Freezing. Forgot to leave the paraffin heater on, didn't I. Burn the bloody house down while you're at it, why don't you. Wino-like, we both tumble down. And perhaps recite some blurred conversation. Now you're over there all wrapped up in your camouflage army surplus, and I'm over here on civvie street. Do you know what it's like to go to bed with all your clothes on? A mixture of ice-cold laziness has me clad in thermals (the ones that your mother gave you), socks, sweater and underneath a Donald Duck T-shirt. And really it was stupid. I mean sleeping close by, together, would have made sense for reasons of warmth if not for those of intimacy. And maybe in that warmth we could have discovered, well, something. Each other. Me. Well, like I say we're not lovers, Adam and I. Stupid common sense prevails. And the street light patterns are starting to merge and fade. Maybe a voice from upstairs or down. And sleep arrives in. Solo.

White City, three minutes. We were bound for Queensway, to see some friend of Adam's. This is one of our favourite parts of town, a favourite haunt. All those delicious big white Bayswater Road houses. They dwarf us. We let them. Maybe we both dream of living down here, removed from the half-life that we have strayed into. And sometimes find we like. Adam's friend wasn't in, so we hung around.

We were lazy buggers, Adam and I, for a while. We did stuff, nothing in particular. We did it all the time. That was our friendship. Squatting uses up a lot of time, all those meetings and stuff, all that while together-in-community. When Adam arrived in the other day he seemed extra pleased with himself, chuffed. Good news, he said. In a childlike way he believed that his good news could also be mine, vicariously. Often it was. He said that he had got a job. A job in Pizza Hut. It's not great, he said, but I get my meals. I knew that it would just be a matter of time before he arrived in some day with even better news. And that day came sooner than I thought.

Now I still live here on Tollington Road. And Brigette still lives downstairs. Chris – well, we haven't seen him for weeks. I got the window fixed the other day. And I've got a gas heater now, I prefer the smell of gas. I've held on to the paraffin one, Mr Khan down at the shop said it could be worth something. Yesterday I went over to Queensway. Adam has moved into a flat there with his friend. He is now dating some girl. And when I called over he said that they were getting married. Later, I realised that it was April Fool's Day. He said he might be able to get me a job, a job in the Hut.

HINDERED IN THE INTERVAL

Anthony Newsome

ANTHONY NEWSOME
Anthony Newsome first started writing short stories while studying at the Dublin School of English. Since then he has had a number of articles published and is currently shaping up to unleash his first novel.

A peculiar feeling has crept into this day; emotions are flying through my head causing ephemeral glances back into my youth. I am determined to elucidate on the reasons why and that in itself is somewhat scary. It all started on a Friday in September, nearing the close of the Eighties. A bad eye infection which limited my vision and, even worse, prevented me from applying a thick layer of blue Revlon mascara to both eyes, caused me to shuffle down to the GP clinic. The doctor issued forth a prescription cream that abated my plight. Another day turned into a very irritating little skin rash on my upper body; again the doctor prescribed ointment. I had no idea as to the reasons why my torso was decaying. I went for a blood test. The day the test results returned I went to my boudoir and lay on the carpet, then I gathered all my precious little trinkets and *objets d'art* into the centre of the room to surround myself. There I was, wearing shoulder-pads, milling my way through a litany of after-thoughts, clutching desperately to the past. Striving to sustain a feeling of complete gravity while musing over a plethora of plastic rubbish and items of absolutely no worth whatsoever, which spanned ten years of existence. Inanimate objects can project happy or sad images, but in all can't ever talk. They are a life in parentheses, hidden away from prying eyes, but each one generates its own memories for me. On this day I felt disjointed, not unbelieving, but words failed me and if anyone expected me to plan any kind of event (not that anyone ever did before) it would have been difficult. Anyway it's not that relentless around here. The whole thing, the comprehension, feeling comfortable with this thing. I am stuck for humour, tickle my mind for a happy memory, something that fuses repartée, but there is nothing I can take from this time and arrange into happy and sad for you. And after what seemed like sixty-five hours of loneliness, that day ended.

I remember the first drag shows I did. With the

soundtrack to *Hawaii Five-0* as my signature tune I performed to at least thirty-six people each night. Braved all obstacles to bring a little sunshine onto the hearts of many a poor deluded fellow. Often my fans would say that I gave too much of my inestimable self. I said to them, 'You are right of course, but this is my crusade.' Like the debutante I plumed and fluttered on stage, wearing a lime-green polycotton, Velcro-edged catsuit. My career, however, was halted in mid-drift while my wellbeing descended into a mortal coil of virulent bugs that hounded my every moment. One early dark morning in the depth of winter, with stalactites forming on the bed frame, I awoke sweating profusely, my body burning up and sore, the sheets needing changing and I a dose of tranquillisers. I sat for a while watching the clock, its tick-tock growing in volume. Suddenly I had the clock in smithereens against the wall and without further ado the hanging mirror fell smashing, replicating the clock. Seven years' bad luck, I heard my father scream, but what the fuck, it made me feel better. On waking the next morning I discovered the rash on my chest had assembled momentum and turned into a neon glow. If it had been a tattoo I would have been the envy of any motor-biker club.

Symptoms grew like perspiration on a disco dancer and once again my body was exposed to the medical profession. Mouth ulcers, wheezing, a dry cough that went on and on for a clear month. One day, reclining Bette Davis-style at hospital, a doctor to the right of me (in a Charlton Heston wig) asked me when the vomiting had started. I looked in wonder at this physician and stupidly searched my brain for some coherent answer. I politely said, 'I do not recall.'

What I *did* know chiefly concerned nauseous, queasy mornings which immobilised everything I had wanted to do. I often ate nothing for breakfast and twenty minutes into the morning I had my head in the toilet bowl. Where all the effluent came from I have no idea, because little food could pass these rouged lips at this particular time. Had I been a female in the first throes of pregnancy, judging from the amount of spewing, I would surely have given birth to a baby elephant. I spent whole days literally in the shithouse.

In the hospital a sister nurse with ten-inch talons became a familiar face as did the ward. Yes, in she came with hell behind her, constantly taking various quantities of bodily fluids. Once, when she appeared with a syringe which would seem more conductive to the sedation of polar bears (the thing was enormous), I said, 'Won't you join me for a jab?' I should hate her really. Nearing a three-day stint there, I put forward the idea of drapes and, 'Could the ward porters wear Spandex?' If I had to be there then the place might as well gain a little panache. Is the decision theoretical or practical? To solidify with marching colours the rather bland drabness of grey tubing feeding plasma into various veins around my body. Not very tantalising stuff. But just before I cried out for my Westwood garb, positivity came coursing by, waving an exit sign. My Olympian hospital endurance tests over, I bussed it home. Upon reaching sanctuary I said, 'I'll take a few vitamins to cheer myself up.'

I delved into several health-promoting devices like rekiki, shiatsu, and herbalism in an ardent attempt to stave off illnesses. Sometime in the winter of 1991 the path of spiritualism leapt out at me. Religion was ever present during my infancy; I grew up in a small village on the outskirts of oblivion and every Sunday morning Mother herded us down to the church of the Holy Virgin. The priest, although old, had these gorgeous flowing gowns which were sprinkled with jewellery expensive enough to furnish a small African continent with food and clothing for some weeks. All the teachings of scripture and virtue over wickedness never landed on these cushioned shoulders; nevertheless jogging with Jesus seemed to placate the despair, something to succour me when the deleterious pills ran out late at night. Without thinking about it I said a little prayer before sleeping each night neck-deep under the bed quilt.

I lived in Drumcondra for six years and walked daily to town. One of these short jaunts I entered Switzers' perfume department to view the unaffordable and maybe try a new test product; but all too abruptly, even before I'd passed the first counter, my hand went crazy. It developed a jittery flapping life of its own. Now usually when in the vicinity of designer face-paint my hands would automatically reach out and grab, but on this occasion I followed the offending limb in circles, ending up outside on Grafton Street taking great gulps of air while leaning against a fishmonger's window.

I took to home and the country air of County Wicklow, locking away the party gowns, placing the sling-backs in cold storage and handing out any unused makeup packs at a Tupperware sale in Mrs Flynn's. Summer approached in glory, encouraging foliage to erupt in vivid style. I threw my arms up in the air, laughed out and hugged my mother. Very quickly I settled into the indolent way of rural activities, spending valuable energy on pilgrimages into the agrarian countryside. In time a daily walk through a wood and into the graveyard, where Granny was buried, became a solace; on down through a small village, keeping a weary eye on my Alsatian dog which spent his entire holiday lurching from one pole to another, constantly urinating. My own chemical imbalance ticked on like a funeral cortege. Nobody in the family was told; in fact I don't recall sitting down with a hot cup of Earl Grey and divulging this tale to anyone. Blinded with hazy tiredness I traversed the high roads and byroads in the garden of Ireland, preceding my ascent, once again, into the dizzy heights that were Dublin town. I was no sooner off the bus when the Kryptonite effect of immune breakdown resurfaced, bringing Nirvana closer. I was told to expect more physical problems and wondered how this five-foot nine-inch frame could accommodate them.

Unlike the flirtatious butterfly in the pink cluster of a rose that I once was, my aurora borealis has decreased into an

Hindered in the Interval

incandescent ember. A drifting outlaw has entered a sea of arteries to chart my body like a map. Swirling between every fibre, superseding, circumventing bodily circular matter, hiding out in fertility, living in broken skin, exposing itself to the very life force that straddles two hundred and fifty-six bones. I look back to the illusion of yore and cry.

What is there left to say? I will not delve too much into private matters. My introductions should have started with my boyfriend. We've been lovers for three years now; he has his own flat in Fairview. While in his presence everything is infectious, every day is totally exhausted, then at home I fall into bed and sleep until dawn.

Through the window raindrops slide off silken flower petals and I am left here with reality. Jesus, I am really, really, feeling sick now and I have a few buckets strategically placed round the flat to puke in. I'd imagined always being strong, never allowed myself a minute to concentrate on death. It's only for the old, they say. But what is there to it? You just lie there and let it happen. Surely it can't be any worse than wearing your mother-in-law's cast-offs.

Vera Versatile said that my restlessness comes from 'not sticking to the wholeness regime and eating proper'. I responded with the immortal line, 'A diet.' If you could imagine someone from Ethiopia making the same statement, then no wonder Vera returned from the kitchen clutching enough delf to fill a dishwasher. We chatted. I remarked if the shadows that creep behind catch up in some uncertain place then I will immediately throw out a silken hand for the galloping horseback riders who come from Valhalla, dressed in muscle-rasping velvets, to clasp me up and continue on their quest. That would be a sufficient exit. Yes, a credible puissant ending. By then regrets shall no longer count, but perhaps one, and that being that I did not promenade the church aisle attired in sequins at Confirmation.

WATLING STREET BRIDGE

Keith Ridgway

I stood on the bridge before dawn with the rain hitting my face, and I stared into the river, waiting for something to occur to me. That was why I stood there. It is in such situations that the great moments come. I have read about it. Some conclusion is reached, some decision is made, some revelation settles at the corner of the mind and is slowly lit, like the sun that grows out of the cold ground in the east.

But nothing came. I felt the rain break the banks of my eyebrows and drip from my lashes and run down my cheeks. It worked its way into my ears somehow, so that I had to tilt my head to one side and knock the heel of my hand against my temple. It ran down my chin, to my neck, disappearing beneath the layers of my clothes. I could feel the rain on my chest. I could feel the rain inside me. I cannot explain that.

Below, the water swirled darkly, the rain and the street lights making it glisten a little; choppy like a landslide of black rock, running like the blood of a cut.

Nothing happened. Everything stayed the same. The same twisting of the heart, as if blind hands were attempting to wring it dry. I could not tell what it was, what name to give it. Sorrow does not cover it, but despair would be too strong. And there was anger there too; a background but distinct rage, like a razor-sharp knife wielded in the distance – thin lines of sudden red, and a sound with it, a night-time tearing.

I have done nothing wrong. It's not like that. I have committed no sin – at least, none to speak of; and certainly I have committed no crime. Not lately. Not that I know of. But I am struggling with hindsight, and regret has placed a hand on me, and a dim shadow has loomed up in front of me, and I am seen by strange eyes and I know not the reason.

Eyes, I said. Grotesque and familiar. I know the reason.

There are cars that go by, taxis mostly. I'm sure the drivers think that I'm going to jump. But it's not that. That is not in my nature.

When my lover threw me out, he did so without anger. He was calm and practical. I stood there in the street with things neatly packed, all my belongings piled up and labelled, boxed and retrievable. The items I might need were close to hand. The heavy stuff was distributed cleverly, so that I could lift every package single-handed. It was as if he wanted to emphasise something. I did not need help.

And he was right to throw me out, and he was wrong. But that comes later. Firstly, there were the good years, and then there just years, when we knew about the future because it was the same as the present. We had passed from the comfort of believing that we were safe from ourselves, and moved into a bleaker place. We began to look at the ground and kick up dust and stumble half-heartedly over whatever obstacles we could find in the empty spaces that surrounded us. We sought out ways of getting lost. We tried to walk in perfect circles, to come across footsteps that we could recognise as our own. There was nothing in the way of pain that we did not taste for the simple sake of tasting it. We were trying to break the skin that held us – or rather, we were trying to see if it could hold. We played with sharp strings and the pointed turning of minutes, watching each other constantly, as a gambler watches God and hopes that God is watching. It was not good.

In the late afternoon I came home to find him with another. I had expected it. They lay sleeping, wrapped up in each other in a way that suggested practice. I pulled the covers from the bed and sprayed the soft white foam of a fire extinguisher on their bodies. There was a loudness then, and a blur of white panic like the frantic thrashing of birds thrown down in a storm. They struggled and spluttered, trying constantly to rise, but slipping back against each other until I thought that they would drown. I stopped then.

His friend had to shower before dressing. I watched him standing in the bath, running his hands over the kind of body that I could never have had. He looked at me and cursed under his breath, but he continued, and did not turn away. My lover meanwhile cleaned himself with towels, and put on his dressing gown, and lit a cigarette, and sat on the edge of the bed, surveying the mess with disdain.

I watched the stranger get dressed. I followed him out of our flat and down the stairs to the street, and I followed him all the way into the city centre and watched as he climbed, nervously, on to a number 16 bus. Then I went and got drunk, and I did not go home for a week. I stayed with friends and told them nothing. I went to work as usual and did the best I could. He did not ring. He did not look for me. I supposed he did not care.

When eventually I returned, it was with the intention of simply gathering my belongings and moving out permanently. But I was greeted with tears, and with remorse, and with the assurance that the man who had slept in my bed had been a 'necessary failure'. That the 'whole mess' has served only to enable a realisation on the part of my lover that I was the man for him. The only one that mattered. The love of his life.

I should have seen it for what it was. But I did not. I saw only my home, and my lover, and the years that we had notched up together, and I folded and I threw in my hand. I slept that night like a child sleeps, possessed of a security that is not of this world. In my mind I herded my fears into a circle and called it 'the bad patch', and I carried on.

We moved out of this bleak region for a while. We travelled through a different place, where we reckoned ourselves stronger, wiser, closer. We strode. But it did not last. Eventually we became self-conscious, and needed to concentrate to keep our footing. And then our concentration began to slip, and we with it. The silence returned, and the watchfulness.

I felt myself drawn to the clearly structured tedium of work. I stayed late and did more than I was asked to do. To my surprise I began to enjoy it. Tentatively, they began to give me more responsibilities. After some months they promoted me. They even gave me a raise. My lover observed it all with bemused disinterest. He carried on as he always had. What he did with the extra time which he now had to himself I have no idea. There was nothing to suggest that he saw anybody else. Perhaps he just covered his tracks. Perhaps he simply enjoyed his own company, as I enjoyed mine. We did not socialise. We stopped making love. We stopped touching. Eventually we stopped talking.

I have never understood those straight couples who speak of their children as the means by which their marriages survive. I do not believe them. It is fear that keeps most relationships together, straight or gay. Children might deepen the fear, but that is all. We dread the end of everything.

My lover and I had failed. We were no longer lovers. We were not even friends. We lived together still, and were referred to by others as a couple. But we had failed. And yet we continued. We could not stop. We could not settle it. We could not even mention it. It was as if we were involved in some shameful conspiracy that necessitated our silence on the only thing on which we really agreed. We waited patiently for one of us to make a mistake, to break this tortured, wordless agreement that has us tied to parallel train tracks like two helpless, fluttering, silent movie starlets.

If I could talk to him now.

It was me of course. I was the one who finally did it. I can no longer remember why. Perhaps I did not decide to do it, perhaps it just happened. But I don't think so. I remember only a weight on me, in the middle of winter, like the cold that presses the ground to creaking. I just stood up.

There is a small guesthouse on Gardiner Street that I had passed every day for nearly fifteen years on my way to and from work. I had seen it repainted, seen its name changed at least twice, seen the double glazing go in and the neon sign replaced by something more 'discreet', more fashionable. I had seen the old panelled front door discarded and its place taken by a revolving contraption of tinted glass and bristled edges. And I had seen that out as well, replaced this time by an imitation of the original, painted white, with a brand new brass knocker from Lenehan's. £15.99. I've seen them.

It was a bitter night. The darkness had been dense and complete since five o'clock, and the cold had stretched itself evenly over the city, forming frost on everything that did not move. I was making my way home, clutching parking metres as I skidded slowly along the empty pavements with one eye on the look out for a taxi. I stopped by that white door, and without really thinking about it, I rang the bell. I waited to be admitted, stamping my feet like a soldier.

I do not know what it was that was in my head as I stood there. I cannot remember what I thought about, if anything. I have no recollection. It seems to me now that I must have had some idea of what I was doing. But I remember only the cold, and the smile of the woman who opened the door, and the roaring fire inside, and the hot meal, and the bed where I slept undisturbed until dawn, when I awoke with the clear knowledge that I had stepped, however accidentally, out of the lie. I knew that he would be worried. And I knew that the first thing that would cross his mind would not be that I had been involved in an accident, or had come to some harm, but that I had stayed the night with somebody else.

I went to work that day in the same clothes I had worn the day before. In the evening I went home. He asked me where I had been. I told him that I'd stayed with a friend. That was all. The next day I took a small bag with me, a change of clothes, my toothbrush and razor, and stayed again in the bed-and-breakfast with the white door. The next day he did not ask.

So it went on. I would stay out there, sometimes four nights a week. My lover said nothing. He would look up at me when I came in, as if startled. Then his gaze would return to the television, or the newspaper, or his book. There were moments when I glimpsed the truth of what I was doing. Moments when I caught his eye, just briefly, in passing, and I was able to see, as clear as a cut on white skin, the pain that I was causing. I remember smiling at those moments, taking that pain and tucking it away somewhere inside myself. I thought I did not love him.

You know what happened. I have already told you. I let him assume that I was having some kind of affair. I let him tell people about it. Slowly our friends gathered around him, protecting him, holding him, staring at me with hard eyes. Some of them tried to talk to me. They made the assumptions anyone would make, and I did not correct them. There was no difference. They tried to tell me what it was that I was doing. I heard the words, but I did not listen. Rain on the roof. The words stayed with me. But it was not until years later that I listened to them.

I felt no fear. I felt a kind of rush, an energy, a pulse that joined my own and drove me on. I could not have stopped. I smiled at everything.

My lover found strength somewhere. He lifted the world and flung it. I came home to find my bags packed, cardboard boxes already lined up in the street, a small van hired and waiting, a friend expecting me with a room cleared and a fridge full of beer. Even then I smiled.

There were the practicalities. I had to find a new place to live. I had to sign the documents to allow the sale of our flat. I had to move, to settle. I rented a place in Phibsborough, near the prison. It was a small cottage, one of a streetful, recently modernised and very expensive. I decided that I would not go out much.

At first there was the novelty of it all. The long hours, rooms of my own. I spent my spare time buying second-hand books and watching television. I bought a video recorder with borrowed money and taped late-night films. I began to watch sports. I had never done that before.

It was a Tuesday night, about two months after my lover had thrown me out. I had seen him only once since then, when we had met in the solicitor's office, like a married couple, to sort out the legal situation. He had barely looked at me. I glanced at him, at the side of his face, pale and drawn and tired. I had realised then how old we had become. Since then, nothing. I had not thought of him. Or I had not realised.

I came in from work and I was, for a moment, surprised that the house was empty. It was as if I had forgotten. I had to stop, to stand in the hall in the silence, and work it out. It took only a moment, but it was as if it was the first time I had thought of it. I realised that it was over. I lived somewhere else now. I would not see him again. I had lost him.

I remember that my eyes opened wide, and my hand went to my mouth and my bag fell to the floor. I remember that I gasped and I stumbled forward and I thought that the sound in my throat meant that I was going to be sick, but it did not. I found my way to the bathroom and leaned over the sink, trying to swallow and trying to close my eyes.

A roar came out of me, starting quietly like a moan, and building up steadily, howling, like a steam kettle, spitting tears against the mirror, twisting the skin of my face and clenching my fists to the smooth enamel of the sink until something somewhere had to burst or tear, until eventually I felt the ripping deep inside me, and I felt the strength and the pulse and the energy go out of me as surely as if the air had left the room, and with the same sucking sound as my mouth now made, the water running down my face like the undertow on a rain-soaked beach when the tide has turned and something on the horizon has moved, and the light is somehow different, like a light that is going out.

It started that night, and it has not stopped.

I tried to see him, but nobody would tell me where he

was. I gave them messages for him. I asked for him to call. I invented emergencies, dilemmas, problems with the sale. He would send someone else. After a while he sent no one, he just ignored me.

I wrote letters and gave them to our mutual friends. In them I said that I needed to talk to him, that I thought a terrible mistake had been made. That I could explain. That I had not had an affair at all. I told him about the bed-and-breakfast, about the woman, how she would remember me. He should go and see her. I said sorry. I filled pages with the word, like a schoolboy doing lines. There was no reply. Eventually his friends refused to accept any more. They said that he would only accept letters sent to his solicitor's office.

I went there. I took a day off work and sat in a coffee shop across the street. I felt like Humphrey Bogart. He did not appear. I wrote a dozen urgent letters and posted them the following Monday morning, took the week off work and sat drinking coffee all day. I saw the solicitor come and go. I saw his secretary. She came to the coffee shop for lunch. I saw his clients, men and women who took deep breaths before going through the door. On the Wednesday I thought I saw my lover, but it was not him. He was not my lover.

I thought of breaking into the office. I thought of the tools I might need, of the layout, the location of the files. I tried to remember. Then I thought of buying the secretary lunch, of winning her over, asking her for a small favour. But she would recognise me. She would know what I was doing.

One Friday I stood in the street. I paced up and down in front of the door and waited for the solicitor to appear. It rained on me. He arrived at midday and he said hello without recognising who I was. He would tell me nothing. He said simply that my lover no longer lived in Dublin, and if I had to get in touch with him at all, then I should leave a message and he would pass it on. Where did he live then? The solicitor looked at me as if I was mad. He shook his head. Was he still in the country? He laughed and nodded and turned and pushed the door open with his shoulder.

I tried visiting our old friends. Some of them asked me in. If they left the room I would rummage in drawers and handbags. I would take trips to the bathroom via bedrooms and studies, speed-reading address books, scanning the pages of diaries. I could find nothing. I rang up and tried to get their children to give me the number. All our friends' children were too polite, too well-trained. They told me they'd give their mummies a message.

I began to take trips down the country to the places we had visited together. I tried asking around. I went into post offices and mentioned his name. It was hopeless, and it was not long before I gave it up.

There were problems at work. I could not concentrate. I refused to do overtime of any kind and left promptly each evening at five. In the mornings I slept late and did not arrive until half-nine, or sometimes ten o'clock. My boss took me aside and asked me whether there was a problem that I wanted to talk to him about. For a moment I considered it, but then shook my head and smiled at him. He warned me. He told me that I was not performing. He told me that I was not inexpendable; that although I was good at my job and had given good service, I was not going to be carried. He told me that I must make an effort. He told me that I should tell him if there was a specific problem. He could help me with it. But if there was not, then it was up to me to prove that I was still worth employing.

There is nothing in the language of business that allows an explanation. There is no facility for this. It is outside the range of two suited men in an air-conditioned office overlooking the river. It cannot be expressed in terms of units, of figures, of input, output and margins. I know that he was making an appeal to me on another level. I know that he was reaching out a hand, in his way. But there are different languages in our lives. On one extreme there is the language of the work place, and on the other there is the language of our hearts. There are no shared words.

I could not perform.

It took another six months before they fired me. I tried, for a while, to concentrate, to get things done, to restore some kind of confidence. But I was being closely watched and I could not stand it. In the end it was a missed day that did it. I had stayed up the night before, drinking, writing letters that I could not send, listening over and over again to certain records. I did not fall asleep until dawn and I slept all day. The next morning I arrived at work to find a note on my desk summoning me. I was given a cheque and told that there would be no need for me to work out my notice. By lunchtime I was at home again, slightly confused, hung-over, unemployed.

I cannot remember now how long it took before everything was gone. I don't think it was more than a year. I did all the wrong things. My money was spent on drink. The rent was overdue. I took what benefits I could get, but even with the help they gave me, I could not keep the house. I moved up the road to a bedsit beside the church. From my window I could see into an alleyway where couples went at night.

I did not think of looking for work. A few old friends found me and talked to me. They offered to help. They told me that I was sliding into self-pity, that there was no point to it. I listened to them and nodded. For weeks afterwards I thought my lover would come. I thought that he would hear how bad I was and that he would feel something and that he would come to me. He did not.

I did not wash. I slept and drank, drank and slept. I sold the video recorder and the television. Even then I found it hard to pay the rent. The woman from the Health Board who visited me every month asked me whether I had any family. I thought for a moment she meant my lover. I almost told her that yes, I did have a family, but he had left me. Then I realised what she meant. I have no family.

Watling Street Bridge

The drink got me evicted. I was always drunk, or at least hazy. I had no money. The landlord had been patient, but he could not put up with it any longer. I found myself suddenly homeless and suddenly sober and suddenly scared. I had everything I owned in a dirty suitcase. I kept on thinking that I must have left some things in the bedsit, or in the house, but I had not. Everything was sold.

For two nights I wandered around the city, penniless and frightened. I did not know where I could go. There were no friends left. I collected my dole and looked for a cheap bed-and-breakfast. I remembered the place on Gardiner Street with the white door, but I could not afford it now. I went to the Health Board and asked the woman what I should do. She sent me to the hostel. The hostel by the bridge.

They told me that there was no drink allowed, and they took me in and gave me a room that overlooked the rushing water, and the rain that dripped from the green-painted ironwork of Watling Street Bridge. I remembered it then. I looked out of my window and I remembered.

It had been a summer's day when we were still young, still in our twenties. We had walked from O'Connell Street, down along the river's edge, talking to each other, taking our time, finding things out. It was not long after we had first met. We walked as far as Heuston Station, where the road leaves the riverside and disappears into the suburbs. We had turned then and walked back, first on the quay down which we had come, and then crossing Watling Street Bridge to the other side. We stopped in the middle to look down into the water, the hazy green water that lapped gently at the old stone. We stood side by side, our arms touching, our elbows on the parapet, feeling the breeze on our skin. My lover turned to me and took my head in his hands. He kissed me. At first I was afraid. There were cars on the bridge. There were people walking. But he kissed me again, and I closed my eyes, and slowly I wrapped my arms around and knew, calmly, like an adult comes to know these things, that there was nothing that could be done, ever, to take him from me.

I do not drink now. My head is clear. I am sober like the iron, like the rain that runs down my face, like the lessening of the darkness that struggles out of the east. There has been no sign.

I have waited for something else to come into my mind. I have expected it. It is not sensible for me to stand here and wait for my lover. I know that there is something about it that is not right. Each night I hope that he will come, and I hope that I will cease to care. But when I think about it, a pain starts inside me and I know that it is the only thing. It is what I am, there is nothing else.

Today, if they let me, I will get some sleep in the hostel and eat their food. While I do that, they keep an eye out for me, in case he comes. I know some of them say they will and then do not, but some of them understand, and they watch, and when I get up they shake their heads.

I know that one day he will come here. I know that he has forgotten, or is trying to forget. But one day something will happen and he will remember, and he will make his way to where I am. He will be old by now, like I am. But he will not die before I've seen him again. He will not.

It is a simple thing that keeps me. It is love.

NEAR THE BONE

Cherry Smyth

CHERRY SMYTH
Cherry Smyth was born in northern Ireland and now lives in London. She has published poetry and short fiction in several anthologies. She is also the author of Queer Notions, *published in 1992, a book charting the rise of urban queer culture. She performs regularly on the poetry circuit and in 1993 won second prize in the London Writers' Competition with her poem 'The Dinner Dance'. She is currently working on a book of short stories.*

I only come back once a year if I can help it. Cootehill, County Cavan, where even the faded postcards, if you can get any, can't make it look special. It is not a 'must see' town, hasn't acquired enough heritage to build a centre. There's a wide main street with several pubs, two pharmacies, a post office and a two-star AA hotel – the White Horse Inn. I used to dream that I could come back and be able to stay in that place for as long as I liked. Buy it even. Instead I went to Germany to work in a printing works one summer and that was that. The hotel went rapidly downmarket and now is kept running on functions, not guests.

I walk down Bridge Street past clumps of teenage boys hanging out on the corners. Apart from the video shop my mother mentioned, there's just as little to do as when I was young, itching to leave, scornful of anyone who stayed stuck. The smell of singed kebabs leaks out of Giovanni's takeaway, masking the sweetness of turfsmoke. Shankey's supermarket has a spanking new front, and a couple of farmhands perch on the high, pink stools in Paddy's Diner, waiting for Demi Moore to waltz in and make their day.

I find myself in the West End Bar which hasn't changed at all. My eyes take a moment to grow accustomed to the dimness. The faint tangerine glow from the tinted windows always made me think of the rusty water that seeps out and collects in narrow ditches in the bog. The bar still smells the same, like any other – spilt beer, fag-ends, sweaty leatherette, the motionless air laced with the acrid whiff of industrial toilet cleaner, which must eat through enamel. I don't know why I go in there, especially in the afternoon. Most of the people I knew have moved on, to Dublin, London or America. Or else they're married with three kids, a half-finished bungalow, with a swing and a cement mixer in the garden and two eagles mounted on the gateposts. Those guys only come out for stag nights and the World Cup.

I always take my earring out and shave off my moustache before I come home. Nonetheless, I still sense that they know I'm different as I walk stiffly to the counter. I don't really drink any more, it's just for appearances and some kind of nostalgia. Though why I'm nostalgic for this place I'll never know. Much of my time in here I spend bluffing. Pretending to fancy Micky's sister, Gerry's cousin, so and so's bloody unmarried aunt. Flirting heartlessly.

'Hey Desi, how's about you?' calls Malachi, the barman. He's greyer on top. They're friendly alright. My shoulders ease a little. I work out in a gym in Frankfurt. I don't even wear a tight T-shirt that would show it off. Truckdrivers round here would have muscles like mine, but if they thought I went to the gym, they might twig.

'The family well?' Malachi dries his hands on his jeans.

'The best,' I supply, the ritual coming back to me with every gesture, every glance. I order a pint and look around, nod at an old school friend I never liked. There's a poster of a red Ferrari on the wall. No one in Cootehill will ever touch inside one, I think sourly. The Triaxles are playing tonight. Then Susan O'Kane tomorrow. I can't believe she's still around. Didn't she sign a record deal?

The pub is quiet, the pool tables waiting and the jukebox silent. It's early yet. Kevin Mulligan's elbows are pinned to the other end of the bar, his face red and pocked, his eyes blue as morning glories. Someone should tell him not to wear a red jacket. He looks as though he is about to smoulder and combust, nose first. Suddenly I imagine him head-to-toe in leather, a Muir cap jammed on his head, and the rush of cruising teems through me like amyl nitrate. I want HiNRG streaming through my muscles, making space between the bones, till they loosen, follow the beat, pull me away from the dark walls into cones of coloured light on the dance floor. Ultra-violet would bathe me till my T-shirt would be radiant, my skin bronzed. The pleasure of being watched would pump me up till I'd be surrounded by an electric band of gazes and the exhilaration of knowing anything could happen. My ears would buzz with the volume, my nostrils embrace the bitter sniff of poppers and sweat. Every pore would focus on desire, taste it in the quick dart of an eye, a glance returned, touch it in the anonymous fondling of men's faces, cupped tits and neat arses. My body would be young, made beautiful, sensuous as a stallion.

I take a gulp of Guinness, lift and adjust my balls, smiling to myself. Here men over twenty-five dance only at weddings.

I study a middle-aged couple sitting in a corner, not talking, staring at the blank TV screen. I recognise them, but have forgotten their name. McConkey, is it? I'll ask Malachi. The man lights one Major after another and each time his wife slides the green and white packet to her side of the table, admonishing him with a roll of her eyes. There are three women on their own. I can tell by their lack of interest in each other, then their sudden, giddy intimacy, that they are family. A mother in purple, the two daughters in peach and cerise. All the same jumper. Dunnes Stores.

My sister never comes back. She's in Newcastle-Upon-Tyne. It would cost her less then me to come. She and our mother fell out over clothes. I tried to keep out of it. Bernie said it was plain fucking crazy, there she was wearing a tie-dye vest which showed her black bra straps and Mum went loopy, calling her a hoor as she went out the door. 'Have you no shame? Someone'll grab you,' she warned. 'It's as if people aren't meant to know I fucking wear one for Chrissakes.' Mum never liked her swearing. It got worse in England. I never swear in front of Mum. What's the point in upsetting her?

I spin the cardboard Harp coaster and wait for someone I know to come in. If not, I'll go home, spend the evening reading the paper, watching the box, while Mum and Dad blather on again about who's sick, who's dead, God love them.

The door opens and Flinty McClure comes in. He was several years ahead of me at school, but we both played football for the County. He rushes right over and shakes my hand, asks me what I'm having. He's more friendly than I've ever seen him, his big red mane of hair as wild as ever, his teeth stained yellow. He's lost weight.

'Still writing the poetry then, Flinty?'

I sound more jocular than I feel.

'Aye.' He shakes his head. 'Not so much lately though.' At once the energy of his greeting has evaporated as though he has been exhausted by it.

Unsummoned, Malachi places a large malt in front of Flinty, who reaches into his pocket. Malachi waves his hand to stop him.

'Catch yoursel' on,' he scolds kindly.

'And you're getting back into shape, I see.' I stand upright and pat my firm stomach.

Flinty sips his whiskey, says nothing. He brings out the old lighter that gave him his name, thumbs the wheel and sucks a cigarette into life. He points the packet towards me. I decline.

'And where's Bob Breen?' I go on as though there's been no break in the conversation. Bob and Flinty always drank together. Bob plays the pipes.

Flinty's face collapses a little. He doesn't look at me.

'Did you not hear, Desi?' He inhales again as if to pump his lungs with courage and turns to me.

'Bobby's dead these three weeks.'

'Sure I never heard,' I protest lamely. 'My mother and father tell me nothing.' I am trying not to look into his eyes. I don't know whether to say I'm sorry. I say it anyway.

'What killed him?' I ask gently.

He hesitates.

'Cancer.' His voice is hoarse.

I tell him I think it's awful and it's Sellafield and pollution and it must be hard for him drinking alone.

Flinty swirls his drink round in its glass. He has a deep cut on his hand which is not healing. Pale green pus lines its edges. A Paul Brady track breaks out of the jukebox. It takes me back. I am relieved when Flinty changes the subject.

'So you're doing well in Germany, is it?' He clears his throat.

'Well enough. It's not Ireland though.'

'You'll be getting married out there soon.' He sounds matter-of-fact.

'Soon enough.' I look away and catch Malachi's eye, tilting up my almost-empty glass. I fidget with the little finger of my left hand, where I normally wear a ring. I twist the bare skin.

Flinty's sadness is upon him like a big, sulky animal. It sucks in all the air between us until I feel as though I will suffocate unless I move away. I don't encourage him to stay for another when he knocks back his short and says cheerio with pretended brightness. He coughs a loose phlegmy cough, peers round the bar, taps his pockets as if he's lost something, waves to Malachi and walks away. His clothes look too big for him. Crumpled.

Malachi comes up to serve me. 'Same again?' I slide my glass towards him.

'Terrible sad,' he mutters, gazing at the door.

'No one said at the funeral and we don't let on we all know.'

He lowers his voice, leans towards me.

'Bob had AIDS.' There is sorrow but no fear in his words.

I gasp through my teeth involuntarily and bend my head into my hands.

'Jesus, I –' My voice dissolves. I didn't know, couldn't have known. Why didn't I comfort the man? I didn't even see him. Christ. Into shape. What in God's name made me say that? I think of my father suddenly. I remember a rare time I went for a walk with him. Up to Annamaghkerrig. It was cloudy but the rain of earlier had eased off. The air was still. He didn't talk much but there was less distance between us then. I lived at home and was uncertain of my desire, not yet guilty of having acted upon it. When we climbed the little hill above the lake he stopped.

'Look,' he said.

I gave a bored mumble. The lake was a round grey stone, the trees sloping up the hillside opposite were green. The water was flat. The arc of trees was mirrored on its surface in sharp, jagged dark and light lines. It was not until later as we walked into the woods and I looked back on the lake that I realised how perfect the reflection had been. A flag of small ripples had scattered the crisp glassiness, blotting and fragmenting the image. I hadn't seen what Dad had meant until it was too late to share it.

Malachi asks me if I'm alright. I nod. He goes on wiping the counter, waiting for my Guinness to darken and settle. His body knows patience.

'Flinty never left his side, they say.' His voice is soft with admiration. He slices the creamy top off the pint. 'Never left his side.'

I feel like I am sinking back into the blackness of the bog, vanishing without mercy into the land that made me believe that I was the only one.

My stomach bubbles and churns. I want to chase after Flinty, explain that I understand, take his big hand in mine, look into the light in his eyes. Tell him about Eamonn, Rudolph, about Timothy and the others.

Malachi pushes the pint towards me and waits for the money.

THE INHERITANCE

Jo Hughes

Jo Hughes
Jo Hughes has had stories published in Spare Rib, Everywoman, Cambrensis, Corridor *and* The Cardiff Poet. *After several years working as a designer in London, she has recently completed a degree. She is currently working on a novel and plans to return to Ireland in August 1995.*

Liam's nickname at school had been Perry. It wasn't until many years after, that he began to understand the full significance of the name. Which was this: Perry Como = homo. He tried to laugh it off, by remembering what his Mammy had told him about nicknames being signs of affection that were only given to popular children. Yet he felt discomforted by it and sensed beneath the laughter, thinly veiled hatred.

He knew that despite his undiluted accent (the family had moved over to London in 1971 when he was fifteen) the teasing had nothing to do with his being Irish. After all, his elder brother was at the same school and his nickname was Paddy – and crude and predictable as that was, it didn't carry the malice and menace of the hated Perry.

Liam was shockingly good-looking. While he himself avoided mirrors, hating the particulars of his features and colouring, women of all ages seemed to respond to him. Girls his own age would blush and giggle when he was near and women in their twenties and thirties would appraise him with frank devouring gazes, and older women eyed him wistfully, as if remembering something undiluted and poignant from back before he wasn't even born.

Liam, it was said, had inherited his gleaming blue-black hair and big dark eyes from his great-aunt Caitlín. She, he was sick of hearing, had been a famous beauty, the toast of Dublin, and Yeats himself was supposed to have once written a poem dedicated to her sparkling eyes. But there was a rise, a climax and a fall to the tales of great-aunt Caitlín. After the talk of the lightness of her step when dancing and the delicacy of her little white hands, there was always a deep sigh and a shaking of heads, then, 'Twas a pity. A blessed pity', and then, 'Poor Caitlín...' After this someone, usually his grandfather, would pipe up with a warning note in his voice and repeat some cliché about 'Beauty paying its price' or 'Pride coming before a fall', or in a gentler mood, his words half-lost in a whisper, he'd say how only the good died young.

Liam and the other children had learned that no amount of questioning or excited clamouring would extract an answer to their pleas of 'What happened?' and 'How did she die?' So great-aunt Caitlín held on to her secrets and took them with her into the muddy waters of the Liffey where, it was hinted, she'd taken her last watery and choking gasps of life.

Liam found the gift of her beauty tainted with the curse of her tragedy. He wished he'd taken after his Uncle Seán with his wall-eye and freckled face and bad breath. Or even Aunt Róisín with her face so flat and round and her nose so small and upturned that Liam's Dad said she looked like someone who'd been whacked full on in the head with a shovel.

Liam looked, more than anything, like he didn't belong to that family, as both his Mammy and his Daddy and all his brothers and sisters had sandy or reddish hair and all had eyes that were quite pale and watery in varying shades of blue and green. They each had fair eyebrows and lashes which gave them a distinctive look, a sort of lack of expression. Liam, in contrast, looked distinctly Mediterranean, as if some angel in a moment of perverse humour had stolen a sallow-skinned baby from its cot in Padua or Tuscany and deposited it in County Mayo. Was there some unfortunate red-haired youth, Liam wondered, growing up in the ancient alleys and backstreets of Italy, forever cursing his freckles and blue eyes?

Perhaps because of how he looked, Liam was always being mistaken for someone artistic – a poet or painter. But this was not the case; he wasn't even one of those people with the yearning to create or perform but none of the talent. Liam had an analytical mind, one full of theories, measurements, comparisons, equations, blueprints and percentage graphs. Thinking about anything that could be

The Inheritance

measured in pounds and ounces, joules or watts, farads or therms, made the world feel good and solid under his feet, while concepts and art forms like poetry seemed to make him feel lost and light-headed – he could not see the point in them.

He could not see the point, especially, in the scribbled or painstakingly penned notes and poems he often found in his desk or sports bag. They would be decorated with flowers and hearts that had been punctured by little arrows and were sometimes anonymous and sometimes signed. They came from Shelly or Julie or Tracy or Cathy. Why, he wondered, as he disposed of yet another note, did all the girls who swore to love him forever have names that ended in 'y'?

Sometimes there'd be a gift along with the note. Back home when he'd been eleven or twelve he'd been given toffees or fruit and once, inexplicably, a Biggles book. But now, just as the shape and look of these girls had changed – with their stockings and high tottering heels and hairspray and cone-like breasts – the gifts had also changed. He'd been given a miniature of cherry brandy which was much too sweet, but he'd drunk it anyway; a small lump of cannabis wrapped in tin foil that he hadn't recognised and so had thrown it in the bin; a David Cassidy single which he'd recycled by giving it to his sister for her tenth birthday; and a well-worn copy of George Orwell's *Animal Farm*. Lizzie Morris, who was reputed to have slept with half the Rolling Stones, as well as David Bowie and Marc Bolan, gave him a pair of knickers. They were made from slippery black nylon material and had details in fraying red lace. The elastic had gone in one leg.

The message that accompanied the last item was as lurid as the gift and the next day, Lizzie had pressed herself up against him in the queue outside the language laboratory and as he registered the two hard points of her breasts meet his shoulder blades, she whispered for him to sit up the back next to her. He didn't and on the way out at the end of the lesson she pushed roughly past him and red-faced, hissed, 'You're fucking dead, McCabe!' He shivered, but it was a shiver of relief. Lizzie's love, he was sure, would have been as crude and violent as her hate, and he'd escaped.

Yet everything seemed to change after that. People suddenly began avoiding him – some subtly, some obviously, overplaying the way they moved away from him, saying loudly, 'I'm not sitting there!' Others were taunted away, afraid of persecution through contamination, and the name he got called changed. It was no longer just the vaguely unsettling Perry (which he'd come to think might have something to do with his Mediterranean appearance); now it was blunt and indisputable: queer, fairy, poofter, bum boy, pansy.

To make matters worse Lizzie got herself a new boyfriend – a skinhead who called himself Kurt because he thought the name sounded strong and Germanic. Liam had once seen him spit in the face of a little Asian girl who couldn't have been more than twelve. Liam had seen it and done nothing, but then there must have been thirty or forty kids in the playground that day who saw it and did nothing. All of them did nothing but shrink away and think themselves lucky that they hadn't received Kurt's special attentions that day.

For a year Liam practised the uncertain art of invisibility and at the same time he tried to come to terms with what he told himself was 'his difference'. If he was what they said he was, then for him it went by another name, but what name that was he didn't know.

One Saturday when he was eighteen, Liam was in town getting some shopping for his mother – his little sister was in bed with chicken pox and she had stayed home to guard against scratching and to apply liberal doses of camomile lotion. Carrying three bags of shopping he'd wandered down a back road in search of a second-hand record shop he'd heard about, when out of the past came a voice that was unmistakable.

'Oi! Perry!'

It was a girl's voice, husky and over-loud – Lizzie's voice. He stopped and turned. Lizzie was half-standing, half-leaning, draped over Kurt and surrounded by six or seven other young men who struck postures which managed to combine both boredom and menace. Lizzie, who'd left school over a year before, looked much older and scrawnier than he'd remembered. He noted that she had bleached her hair white-blonde to match Kurt's and had cut it so that it was no more than a quarter of an inch over her skull, except for a short and curious wispy fringe that fell over her forehead.

'Oi. Come here.' Lizzie smiled as she said it, while Kurt gazed off into the distance, grinning at some private joke.

Liam, after briefly considering flight with his precious cargo of Sunday joint and other essentials weighing him down, walked cautiously over. It had rained earlier and although the sun was now out, the sky was still filled with ominous slate grey clouds and there were few shoppers about.

'Got any money to lend us?' said Lizzie in a tone that verged on sweetness.

Liam hesitated – maybe if he just gave them a few shillings with the pretence of it being a loan that would satisfy them. He reached into his pocket and took out all the money he had, which was one pound note and some change. Awkwardly, as he now held all three bags on one arm, he selected the coppers and offered them to Lizzie.

In the meantime, the group had drawn closer – someone, he sensed as Lizzie reached for the proferred money, was moving around close behind him. 'Come on, mate,' said Kurt who, while he still gazed into the distance, was openly and dispassionately kneading one of Lizzie's breasts, and she was letting him as if it were her knee or shoulder.

Liam was watching Kurt's hand, as one might watch an unusual animal in its cage, when several things seemed to happen all at once. Something pushed him hard on the back of his head, while a foot, which must have been aimed at his genitals, missed its mark and struck his inner thigh. The bags were ripped from his arm, which horrified him more than the sudden violence.

He stood in dazed silence, while they began to inspect the shopping. The onions and carrots and leeks they discarded by lobbing them, frisbee-like, into the road. The shoulder of lamb, his father's stout and his sister's medicine they set aside. Then they came to the packet of sanitary towels his mother had insisted he get for her. These received special attention. The packet was ripped open and the contents waved in his face like terrible flags.

'Jam rags!'

'I said he was a frigging woman, didn't I!'

Later Liam would vaguely remember saying or beginning to say, 'Okay, a joke's a joke...' but maybe that was only something he'd dreamed or overheard when he was unconscious in the hospital. He did remember rain, big thunder drops that splashed on to one side of his face, and something hard and cold was pressed against his other cheek. And he remembered looking with numb fascination at his lower leg which seemed to be bending the wrong way, as if it didn't belong to him at all. He remembered too, the hospital, the urgent crash of equipment, the hurried voices, but perhaps he was getting that confused with something he'd seen on television.

After he recovered, his good looks miraculously unimpaired, he found that his parents had changed towards him. Suddenly he was their 'darling boy' and they treated him as if he was made of china and at the merest touch might break. They were always, for those few days while he sat propped in the armchair in the front parlour with an eiderdown over him, talking about what was best for him.

The Inheritance

And what was best for him, they decided, was to go home.

'But I am home!' said Liam.

'No, no! Back home to Ireland,' they soothed. 'You can stay with your Auntie Mary in Dublin.'

Liam's parents had come to the conclusion – perhaps they had no wish to see it any other way – that he'd been attacked because he was Irish. It had, it was true, been only a month since the big bomb went off in Guildford and in England they all felt a chill wind in its wake.

Liam protested half-heartedly; apart from the family, what was there to keep him in London? And besides this was Dublin that was being proposed – not Limerick or Tipperary.

Mary was Liam's mother's cousin and was a year or so older than her. Mary had been an only child and had never married, staying at home to care for her elderly parents instead. After their deaths she stayed on in the house, which had belonged to the family since it was built in 1879. It was a large three-storey townhouse, but Mary had sold off the two lower floors and now occupied what had once been the servants quarters in the attic. Because of this arrangement most of the good furniture was crammed into the few rooms she still occupied, giving the place an atmosphere of Victorian clutter.

Liam was to sleep on a camp bed in the living room – a situation that forced him into greater contact with Mary than he'd envisioned, but Mary, despite appearances, was a pleasant, witty woman with an easygoing spirit, who was keen to entertain her recuperating guest. She fell only a little short of spoiling him.

Liam's plan was to spend a year in Dublin, then to return to England and begin university, and thus embark on the rest of his life. The future felt rich and full of potential. Everything, he thought, would begin tomorrow.

Mary brought him a cup of tea every morning at nine. He'd wake to the faint clatter of the kettle being put on. He listened as the cup and spoon tattled on the saucer as these were borne towards the room in which he lay. Mary would be half-singing, half-humming 'I Could Have Danced All Night' or 'Molly Malone' or 'The Salley Gardens'. He wondered if she sang just for him or if all these years she had filled the attic with her lonely soprano and sweet sad songs.

During the first week Mary had suggested she show Liam around the city so that he wouldn't get lost in the weeks ahead when he walked these streets alone. But somehow they fell into a pattern of spending each day together.

Into the room she would come and after setting down his cup of tea she would open the curtains and comment on the weather. 'Tis a fine day for a walk in the park.' And so, after breakfast, off the two of them would go. In the evenings they would listen to the radio and while Mary picked up her knitting and began yet another patchwork square (they were to be sewn into a blanket for refugees). Liam would pick up his book about the economic theories of Maynard Keynes and open it at the first page.

Every day for a month he sat with the same book open on his lap and every day he would fail to read more than the first paragraph. It wasn't that Mary's distraction was an unwelcome irritating one; that would have been easy to cope with. No, it was that he loved to hear her talk, to listen to her stories. She kept him entranced by the wealth and depth of her knowledge, with her frankness and bright laughter. It was as if she had stored up all the unspoken conversations of her youth and now they all came rushing out at one.

Liam, who had always been conservative and neat in his appearance, suddenly no longer found the time for going to the barber's once a month. His hair grew and within months it fell over his shoulders in black rippling cascades. Mary said he looked like a wild Irish prince.

One winter evening, when Liam had long given up the idleness of lifting an unread book on to his knees, he and Mary were sitting in the firelight when she suddenly stopped her knitting and said, 'I should show you something – why have I not before?' She disappeared into her bedroom, then returned carrying a small trunk and set it down on the floor in front of the fire.

Together they knelt on the hearth rug and Liam reached forward to open the box, but Mary stopped him. 'Wait,' she said and hurried into the kitchen, coming back seconds later with a very dusty bottle of whiskey and two clean tumblers. She poured each of them a small measure then settled down beside him again.

With great ceremony Mary opened the trunk. Liam peered inside, intrigued by its contents and the importance bestowed upon what looked to him like a collection of old clothes. Mary dug down deep with surety as if she had memorised the exact position of whatever it was she sought. She drew out an album that had been bound in black leather and had the word 'Photographs' tooled in gold on the lower right-hand corner.

Liam drew closer and they sat their backs resting on the settee with the book held between them. The pictures seemed to be arranged chronologically. Liam briefly saw stiff Edwardian figures posed between potted palm and Greek column fly by as Mary turned the pages, searching for the particular thing she wanted to show him.

'Ah ha, here it is!' she said finally. 'Now who do you think that is?'

Liam found himself staring at a black and white photograph of about six by eight inches. It showed a handsome young man, his head turned artfully at the neck, so that he was presented three-quarter-face to the viewer. One large dark and liquid eye looked mournfully out, while the other was half lost in the shadow of a tilted trilby. The shirt he wore was white and crisply starched, the collar stiff and formal.

'Who is he?' asked Liam, feeling a strange mixture of both desire and recognition.

'Wait,' said Mary, turning the page, 'there.'

Liam didn't understand the triumph in her voice – this did not answer his question. Here was another photograph, but it was of a young woman. The pose was similar, yet everything here was softer, feminised. Her eyes, though equally dark, seemed beguiling and a coy smile played at the edges of her lips. Her hair fell in dark glistening waves over the lace of her bodice.

'Are they related?' asked Liam, turning the page to and fro for comparison.

'You could say that.'

'Well, come on, Mary – don't be a tease, tell me, who are they?'

Mary looked delighted. She took a sip of whiskey and smiled. 'That,' she said with evident pleasure at the trick, 'that is your great-aunt Caitlín.'

Liam was about to say 'and the young man?' but the penny dropped before the words had reached his lips. 'Jesus,' he said, then snatched the album to take a closer look, 'that's amazing.'

'Ah, but there's more. Go and look in the mirror.'

Obediently, he stood and, still holding the album, looked first at himself, then at the young man and then the young woman. Then he looked again, and again until all the faces became one. One that was beautiful, neither totally male or female. It was a trick with mirrors and light, yet it was more than that – a melding of souls, an inheritance of difference.

RAINDANCING

Anthony McGrath

ANTHONY MCGRATH
At the tender unripened age of twenty-two, Anthony McGrath wants to hit forehands like Steffi Graf, hold a note like Barbra Streisand, have a walk-in wardrobe like Jennifer Hart and to be a tall, thin, tantalising, tanned one-man man – all of which he is achieving at an inferior rate to that which he deserves. However, he hopes to be a writer whose hopes and visions filter from pen to paper to print to purchasable – and that's the hope on which futures are built.

My mother was not beautiful; only in my eyes did she sparkle like a fine-cut diamond and glow with the warmth of a flickering candle. Her face was plain; only when she dressed it with a smile did features appear upon her like decorations, like a Christmas tree that had just been lit up. That is what I shall always remember about her – above all else, it will be just how beautiful she really was when she smiled.

With each passing day another detail fades like some yellow-tinted black and white, of which there are still so many in some isolated attic crevice that remains to be gone through and dealt with. I don't think I can now remember the exact colouring of her hair, or the style which she chose to wear it in.

My mother always claimed that the death of her own mother, some twenty years earlier, was something she had never gotten over; and never had a single day dawned and died without some memory flooding her mind, however momentarily and however triggered.

We had this glorious relationship that transcended the normal mother-and-son pairings. As a child, we spent our early afternoons doing Parisian things. We walked in the park, pushed ourselves on the swings with youthful vigour; and at the very sight of fine rain, we would hurry out back to spin about the garden, laughing as the rain first dampened, then dripped from us. Knowing no better, I believed that here, spinning with me and laughing as true and as loud as myself, was not just the woman who was my mother, but a person with whom I could forever spin in the rain with. When we would eventually return inside to remove our by now heavy and wet clothing, as she would tenderly towel-dry my hair, we would still laugh – not at our stupidity, but with our joy.

I can never remember my mother shout; I don't think I would recognise her voice if it were raised, nor to be honest, do I think it was capable of being raised. All I know is that when we had our few confrontations, it was the look of disappointment in her vocal eyes that cut deeper and hurt more than any words spoken aloud could achieve, or any raised palm succeed.

I loved her in the blinkered way that only a child can love a mother. I drowned in the freshness of her jumpers, became intoxicated by the fragrance she wore, marvelled at the way she could move with the smoothness of satin. It was a relationship that my elder sister Jane was robbed of, and well removed from, for only the youngest gets the attention in such divine ways, and continues to receive it only if they remain the last born.

No other woman could possibly have given me a happier childhood, or cared for me any better, than she did. I want to say that now, before I tell my story, that she will always be to me my mother – I own her for that, respect her for that, but perhaps I don't love her for it any more.

Jane was eventually stolen by a man, as we always knew she would be, for she had inherited the attractive simplicity of my mother's beauty. What no one knew, or seemingly expected, was that I'd be stolen by one too.

I met Gordon the first day of college. He walked across the cobblestones carrying a worn brown leather attaché case, wearing a maroon corduroy jacket, his hair alive on the fingers of the wind. As we passed, our eyes met for what was, in reality, a mere second, but felt embarrassingly longer. It was a glance that said something, but by now I've seen those same eyes say so much, I can never quite recall what exactly they said to me that day. He walked on by, casual and carefree, and that was that.

We met, quite by chance, in the library four days later when I boldly opted to sit at his study desk. I watched him read until he looked up at me, and then we shared a cigarette over coffee. We went for a drink the day after and within another week, he had taken me to his bed. I was not the first to go there, but from what I know, I was the last. It was there, lying in his arms, full of warmth and security, hearing his heart beat near me, looking up to see his exhaled smoke resting before him like some cartoon bubble, that I realised I had found happiness.

The next few months were special, as special as they can only be to lovers. We made Bewleys for black coffees first thing every morning, we delighted in finding hidden alcoves in lonely restaurants where we could be all we knew we were, where mild music elegantly crept rather than invaded our haven; where we argued politics, discussed news and more importantly, fell deeper in love. It was a love I had known nothing about, one that simultaneously groped me with nervousness and excitement till they became an indistinguishable cohesive whole, equally balanced and enjoyed. At times I felt my smile would gleam itself off my face when I sat across a table from him, happy that the hours I had waited to meet him had elapsed and that the time had come.

I guess I knew I was gay from about the age of fourteen, but the gap between realisation and acceptance took its time. With Gordon, I could accept all that we were, and could see no wrong in it – no harm, no hurt, no humiliation that a media had thought me to feel.

I always knew that telling my mother would be difficult, because there was something innocent about her existence; an innocence I admired and adored. She believed in family units, she believed in a church and she believed in all that the generations gone before had held good. The moral dilemmas of today's society never played on her mind. 'Open minds let in the wrong sort of stuff' was her cast-in-stone motto. At one dinner party, as a guest began to discuss the abortion issue, they promptly cut their speech short at the sight of my mother nervously twisting her napkin in embarrassment.

Yet I had to tell her, to share this feeling that had hypnotised me – and I expected, with all her love, all our past, that she would welcome it. I came home on that short-lived November day, imbrued with a wind so cold, but it was not to be that way, nor should I ever have imagined it could have been so. Her face seemed to collapse, her eyes recede into the distance. I said what I had sat her down to say, and she never once spoke during it, but remained seated where she was, as if frozen. At times, I felt she wasn't even listening. When finally I had finished, she sat for many minutes in silence, forming the words she was going to say with deliberation, and with the knowledge that each one of them would cut me, cut deeper than I though she could ever hurt me. In a few short minutes she had betrayed me and our traditional love. She stood up to go, tears in her eyes.

I sought and found refuge in the arms of Gordon, and it was there I moved permanently. When I made one final visit back to the house to gather and box my belongings, she asked me, without feeling but instead laced with duty, to stay. She said that she could never accept what I'd chosen to become, that we could never mention it again and hope that things might be the same. We both know that things would never be as they once were, we had come to a threshold over which only one of us could go, I could not censor my life for her, nor, having had just spent three sleepless nights in the arms of my lover, could I contain my absolute need for him.

When I left that day, I never saw my mother again. It became a pain that had healed with time. I don't know what Gordon ever saw in me, why he loved me so, but I can only thank God every day for having him there. Over the years, our romance fermented into reality. He cooks, I burn, I clean, he dirties. Our lives have become a variety of bills, discussions on the merits of accepting certain party invites, and refusing others. We have settled into a routine that seldom boasts spontaneous lovemaking; we have become twice-a-week people, with a lovely apartment full of samples from our lives; we have a place and a circle within which we thrive. We have arguments, our once-pure relationship has days of silence, with cursory notes pinned to the fridge by once cute rainbow magnets – but what couples don't?

Twelve years passed without a Christmas card from her, or a birthday gift. I always sent one to her, because you can only silence a love like ours, you can't quite kill it. News of her declining health filtered through in the form of late-night telephone calls from Jane. It began with tests, worked up to cancer, but I never believed that she would die. As the weeks passed, the reports were getting worse. She was riddled, hospitalised, and, eventually, it happened. Jane woke me one morning with the news that the weekend would probably be my mother's last.

The next few days fell upon me with a numbness. I felt that I was walking through a fog, where everything I saw was there but not there. I felt like I was watching my own existence from the outside, that I was not a part of all that was going on about me. I spent dinner arguing with Gordon as to whether I should go and see her, and if she'd lived another week, I probably would have. Funny how in twelve years of living with him, we had never discussed my mother from the time I moved in until it became apparent that her death was imminent.

So now my mother lies dead – we both robbed ourselves of a unique friendship. Should I have compromised to her ideals, or should she have bowed to the source of my true happiness? She never saw Gordon, never gave herself a chance to see all that I saw in him. I think, in hindsight, that she blamed herself for my homosexuality, but what was there to blame herself for? Surely, not happiness.

Perhaps the cost of finding love is another love itself? I will never know, but there is not a single day that now dawns and dies where I don't think about her – not a week I don't place some yellow roses, her favourite, by her tombstone. It is far easier to talk to a mound of clay than to converse with a person. Sometimes I stand there in the wind and cry, but not from love or the loss, because I feel nothing.

All I really know for sure is that I took all the values she thought me into my relationship, my circle and my life, to create one I'm both happy and proud of. If she couldn't be proud of me, I at least hope she's now proud that I'm happy.

Do I love her now? I love what I remember of her, young and spinning in rain; perhaps it is better only to remember that, for then I can say that I love her.

WAITING FOR THE GIRLS

J J Plunkett

Patrick, Jack and I are getting ready to go out. Jack leans over the cluttered dressing table and lip-synchs to the sound of Bananarama – who scream 'Venus Was His Name' from our Amstrad midi-system – while applying dollops of cover-stick to the three small pimples which decorate his chin. He is topless, except for a thin gold cross and chain, which his mother gave to him before he left home, hanging around his neck. His body, though thin and undefined, has a translucent boyish quality that some older men find wildly attractive. It's not my cup of tea though and anyway, Jack goes for older men.

'Jesus H Christ on a bike, I'll never get the shift with my face in this state,' he shouts above the music. 'I thought only adolescents were supposed to get fuckin' acne.'

'Once a spotty git, always a spotty git,' roars Patrick, who is standing in the middle of the room, shaking Imperial Leather talc down the front of his Calvin Kleins. Droplets from his freshly showered hair trickle cleanly down his shoulders and back.

Unlike Jack, Patrick is exactly my type: all taut muscle and blond smoothness, with a tan that glows with golden health, although it's fake. We had it off once, the night we met, but after that he didn't seem to be interested in pursuing the sex thing any more so we became friends and allies in the hunt for men.

I'm lying on the bed beside the window, smoking one of Jack's Marlboro Lights. Although the frenzied activity that is going on around me is a weekend-night ritual, I never get caught up in the rush of excitement that seems very necessary for the other two to begin enjoying themselves. I'm a simple shower, shave, denim shirt, blue 501s and Doc Martens man, the whole idea of dolling myself up leaves me cold. The lads, or girls as they sometimes like to be called, are always on at me to brighten up my image – get a different haircut, a bright red pair of jeans, pierce my ears –

but my unvarying wardrobe has never lessened the interests of men who fancy me, so I feel no need to change it.

I met Patrick at Shaft last New Year's Eve. It was his first time ever to go to a gay club and because his solitary discomfort was so obvious, I honed in on him the moment I saw him. I would like to say I did this out of a sense of sympathy for an uninitiated brother, but the truth is that I found him seriously attractive and I recognised that his unease was the perfect opening for me. I would befriend him and because he would be so grateful for the company, he would be putty in my hands when it came to the question of whom he went home with. Things went according to plan, more or less. All night long I talked with him, standing by the bar, my head leaning intimately towards his in an effort to fend off any other rookies who might take a fancy to him, and by the time the music stopped I was kissing his neck lightly while he nuzzled mine. I took him home and made love to him slowly. He did not make love to me, except to answer my kisses. His body lay prone on my bed as I caressed it and milked it; he didn't once open his eyes or make a sound.

That image of Patrick, all shyness and sad mystery, could not be further from the Patrick who stands before me now. This Patrick is loud and cocky, a big-toothed smile perpetually dances on his lips, and he holds both myself and Jack and an army of lovers and admirers effortlessly in the palm of his golden-brown hand. We are in constant thrall of his every word.

Jack laughs loudly at Patrick's insult and dances over to him to kiss the air beside both of his cheeks.

'Darling, you fuckin' crack me up,' he yells, 'and girl, you don't need Imperial Leather to make that dick come up smelling of roses – bitch.'

I've known Jack for much longer than Patrick; we met almost six years ago at the Youth Group. We were never bosom buddies in those days, but we would pass the time of day politely whenever we met in the Parliament or Bewleys, and we had many mutual friends. It is through one of these friends, Dave, that we ended up moving in together last year. Dave was looking for two other people to share this house and Jack had heard it through the grapevine that I was looking for a place. At first I was wary about moving in with Jack, he is so completely different from me in almost every possible way. He is the epitome of what some personal ads describe unflatteringly as a 'scene queen'. He knows everyone, or at least he knows some gossip about everyone, he is always on show – screaming, jumping, camping it up, talking incessantly – Jack is all fanfare and artifice, he is loved and loathed in equal measure.

His eyes are his saving grace. If you look closely into them you will see hints of vulnerability and innocence, the same qualities that make young children adorable. If you look closely enough at Jack, you will feel the urge to protect him and I suppose that is why we have gotten on so well since we moved in here; I have become his guardian and sentinel. It is a role I have come to enjoy, and a position that Jack appreciates lovingly. He may gossip enthusiastically about everyone on the scene, but he never says a bad word about Patrick or me to anyone. He feels the need to assure us of this fact on a regular basis, to reaffirm our trust in him I suppose.

Dave went to the Mardi Gras in Sydney last March and never came home, so we asked Patrick to move in and take his place. Jack and I were in complete agreement about this decision, in fact we were equally enthusiastic about it. In our own separate ways, I think we are both in love with him, although Patrick seems blissfully unaware of our feelings. Maybe he just ignores them.

Tonight is no different from the countless other nights we have gone out together. We always start the night in this way, the girls in a flurry of preparation, covering blemishes, trying on clothes, blow-drying hair, while I lie around and wait for them. Although I do not partake, I always enjoy. The more excited they become, the more relaxed I become and it is often this way with us. I react to them in reverse mode most of the time. Once we get out, we always make our way to the Parliament first, then on to the George and then on to Shaft or Hooray Henry's to dance into the early hours. We never come home together. Although we seem to be going out to enjoy ourselves, we always have a more urgent underlying motivation – we are on a ceaseless mission to find men.

We are not looking for long-term men, those men that you set up house with and take home to meet your mother. Those men who declare their love for you and promise to take care of you, who neatly infiltrate the structure of your life. Jack and I have known those men and have decided that they are not for us; Patrick has not yet had a chance to experience them and he instinctively knows he is not ready to do so. The men we are looking for can be found leaning against the walls of dark, hot nightclubs, a bottle of beer in one hand, the other hooked by the thumb into the waistband of tight, crotch-hugging 501s. They wear skintight white T-shirts, or sometimes none at all; they occasionally have a nipple pierced. They lean against the wall, feigning confidence, and stare glassy-eyed at you, lightly fingering the bulge in their pants, as you pass by.

When I say that these are the men we are looking for, I mean that they are the men myself and Patrick are looking for. The men that Jack is looking for are of a different sort altogether. These men are the ones that sit at the bar, nursing pints of Guinness, furtively looking at the younger, cocksure men from a more liberated generation. They have beer bellies and defeated eyes, and Jack loves to be loved by them. One at a time though, and no commitments. He is 'seeing' someone at the moment, but that only means he'll go home with him if the night's pickings aren't good.

'Venus Was His Name' comes to an abrupt end and Jack

turns the tape over. Patrick comes over and lies on the bed beside me to take a drag from my cigarette while Abba launch themselves loudly into 'Dancing Queen'. He is still wearing only his Calvins; a thin line of soft golden hair runs down his abdomen, disappearing into the waistband, and I can see the outline of his rosebud cock clearly through the white material.

'Aw, look at the two of ye, ye were fuckin' made for each other!' screams Jack, pretending to take a photograph of us through his fingers. 'Say cheese!'

Patrick goes one better than that and leans up on one elbow to kiss my cheek in the mock pose of an ardent lover. His crotch brushes gently against my leg.

He is always touching us. He rustles our hair, punches our arms affectionately, he comes up from behind and grips us in hugs that leave our arms unable to move. Sometimes when he's drunk, he leans his head on my shoulder, or puts his arms around me and presses his cheek against mine. I have not seen him do this with Jack, but then again, by the time Patrick gets drunk, Jack is usually off flirting with someone else. I want to put my own arms around Patrick, to kiss his lips heavily and let my hand push itself between the warm, dark centre of his legs, but something in his aura gives off a warning signal that such a reaction would not be welcomed. Quite the opposite, there is a sort of veiled, volatile anger about all of Patrick's physicality. If I touched him in return, he might explode.

Jack jumps on the bed with the two of us and shouts, 'Group hug! Group hug!' so we twist our arms around one another and squeeze, all laughter and affection. We are our own little family, we are a small gang of children playing, we are musketeers on an uncharted map; all for one and one for all. 'Charlie's Angels', that's what Jack calls us, three girls together.

There are very few moments when there are just two of us; sometimes late at night Patrick and I talk while Jack sleeps, but as long as he is awake there must always be three. Jack interrupts moments when Patrick and I seem separate to him with laughter and jokes and lighthearted chatter, and he always goes to great pains to include me in anything he and Patrick may be doing together. It's almost as if he is frightened of breaking down the structures of our interconnected relationships, of disturbing the equilibrium we have built up since Patrick moved in. It's an understandable fear and one that I share with him, although to a lesser extent, it seems.

'Hey Jack,' says Patrick, catching his breath, 'run down to the off-licence and get us a few cans of beer. Get the money out of the top pocket in my leather jacket.'

Jack jumps up, as always eager to please, and throws on a T-shirt.

'You two better not get up to anything while I'm gone!' he laughs, popping his head back through the bedroom door, one finger wagging out his warning – and then he is gone and there is just the two of us, lying on the bed.

There is not even a second of awkward silence, not one hint of sexual energy crackling in the air. Patrick lunges. He pins my head to the pillow with his lips, his tongue prizing my teeth apart and assaulting the back of my mouth. His crotch grinds and grows into mine, his cotton-clad buttocks squeezing together in an effort to push beyond the restrictions of his clothing and mine. His hair is still wet and a droplet runs into my right eye. Patrick's own eyes are open and they are like two hot coals burning, not with passion or love or ecstasy – the blaze with barely suppressed rage. My instincts are to push him away, but his body is heavy and my own cock has begun to harden in response to his grinding. His hand pulls my shirt apart and begins to twist my nipples, one after the other and back again.

What can I do? What words are there to say? I put my head back, stretch my arms behind me to grip the headboard and let him bite and pinch and gnaw at my body, let him take my cock roughly into his mouth, his left hand pumping relentlessly on his own.

When I look up again I see Jack's face beyond Patrick's heaving shoulder. He is standing at the door. His expression is one of shocked pain and indignation, like a child who has accidentally plunged his hand into a bunch of stinging nettles while out picking wildflowers. I blink and when my eyes are open again he is gone. I hear the front door slam.

Patrick is sucking and pumping harder and harder, so I lie back and wait for him to come. It takes him a while, but when he does the sounds he makes are like those of a hurt animal. Patrick yelps as he ejaculates. When he is finished, he pulls his face abruptly out of my crotch and makes a dash for the bathroom, still holding his cock, his thick semen dripping down clenched fingers.

Quietly I pull myself up from the bed, buttoning my jeans and shirt. I light another cigarette and lift my coat from the back of the door. From the bathroom I can hear the sound of Patrick retching and I imagine him hunched over the blue toilet bowl.

'I'll meet you in the Parliament in half an hour,' I say, my forehead pressed against the bathroom door. There is no answer. I go downstairs, grab my keys from the hook beside the front door, and putting my jacket on, go out to find Jack.

Tallaght Trash:
The Diary of a Drag Queen

Attracta Cox

Attracta Cox
Attracta was born on a hot summer's day at Dublin Gay Pride in June 1994. After attracting a lot of attention during the parade, she continued to make her presence felt, especially on Sunday nights in a certain Dublin nightclub. She usually surfaces once a week and is proud of her Tallaght roots. She has a severe attraction to shoes and likes to snog a lot of men.

Sunday Morning

'Thank you, Dorothy,' I whispered as I stood in the viewing lobby watching the plane taxi down the runway. My other half had finally pissed off to Santa Ponza with a few of his work (or should I say wank) mates. He would be back on Sunday evening – that gave me a week. The time for major camp had resurfaced after three months of football boots, dirty socks and the smell of Brut, essence of man. Helena definitely made a mistake there.

During that time my wigs, make-up and fabulous apparel had been consigned to boxes at the back of the wardrobe. The raging queen inside was pummelling so hard to get out that my ribs were black and blue. Bruce, my boyfriend, tolerated campness but had a serious aversion to drag. When his mechanically minded mates came around for a few cans of an evening, I was banished to the locked bedroom. Bruce turned up the Phil Collins records to drown out my sobs as I dreamt of escaping to the bedroom and emerging in a lavender skintight PVC catsuit to graciously serve them cocktails.

How I wanted to sing 'Go – walk out the door, don't turn around now, 'cause you're welcome anymore' as I helped him pack this morning. But without Bruce to satisfy my needs my twitching libido would go crazy. The last time he went away for a weekend to Belfast, I wore out three dildos and was contemplating squatting on the knob of the newel post at the end of the stairs. But this time I resolved to keep myself in check and luxuriate in being thin, gorgeous, fabulous, unattainable and even virginal.

Sunday Evening/Night

'Oh, my God, oh my God, oh my God, panic stations!' screamed Agnetha Atrocious as a compact fell to the floor and half its contents left a semi-circular beige smudge on the carpet. 'I should have known better than to buy Constance Carroll pressed powder. One little knock and it's ruined,' she wailed.

'Lancôme sweetie, Lancôme,' a deep voice boomed from the next bedroom. It was BiBi (Bodacious Babs).

'It's all very well for her. She gets all her make-up bought as presents from friends and admirers,' I thought. I myself (Linda Vagina-Blister) use middle-range cosmetics: Yardley, Max Factor and No.7, occasionally stooping to Rimmel and Cover Girl when money is tight. All the while Labia Pissflaps was behind us on the bed trying to put on her tights. We averted our eyes, not wanting to see bollocks at this early stage in the evening. Agnetha and I jostled for mirror space trying to do our foundation. God knows how we always managed to look fabulous considering that one low-wattage lightbulb acted as our illumination.

'Fuck,' shrieked Labia. 'Another pair of tights ripped to shreds.'

She still hadn't mastered the art of putting on a pair.

'Don't worry, you can go as a raped prostitute,' I helpfully suggested.

'No-way – it's the glamour-puss look tonight,' she retorted.

'Dave was summoned from the sitting room. 'Be a luv and get us a pair of Pretty Polly in the Spar on your way back from the office,' she asked graciously.

'Oh, and another bottle of Princess Pippin for me, please,' I said, realising with panic that my second bottle was almost empty.

By the time Dave returned, everybody except *moi* was ready. I needed my eyes done and Dave was the only one who could do them to my exact specifications. Remember I am a fledgling drag queen and I needed all the help I could get. BiBi, in one of her vicious moments, would say I needed serious help, the men-in-white-coats variety, but I disagree. Anyway I already have an excellent psychiatrist.

It was now five to eleven, and after slapping the auburn wig on my head, I was ready. The wig was one of Dave's creations – very Edwardian, swept up at the back with a ringlet at each side and a few at the nape of my neck. With the simple tight black dress and platforms I looked Ab Fab.

Piling into the taxi the driver asked, 'Where to girls?' (No, he wasn't drunk, but it was a particularly dark night.) After looking at each other for a while, Agnetha, the most feminine, stated our destination. Forgetting myself on the way, I made some comment about a cute guy at the traffic lights. The driver's eyes reflected in the mirror said it all. There was total silence until we reached the nightclub. At least his horizons had been broadened.

We strode in *en masse*, causing a few heads to turn. Well, that was the whole point of the exercise, to attract as much attention as possible. Labia and I were at least six foot four in our platforms, so it was hard to overlook us. BiBi led the way to the ladies' loo to do a make-up check. It was difficult not to notice the open-mouthed stares and loud comments, a few hoots of derision, but mostly shouts of 'Work it, girls' as four gee-eyed drag queens sashayed past.

'How do you pout,' I asked BiBi, looking with some worry into the mirror.

'You have to have lips first.'

'Bitch,' I yelled back.

'I knew it, I knew it,' said Agnetha like she had discovered something truly amazing. '"Enough is enough",' she screeched and ran out on to the dancefloor and we stampeded behind, leaping up on stage as it was one of our favourite tracks. I swayed, sashayed, bumped and ground my way through the best the above-average DJ had to offer. When I felt that I didn't get enough attention, Labia and I simulated sex and occasionally I fucked the wall. That seemed to do the trick.

During my second trip to the ladies' I was called 'a dour-faced, silly, prancing ponce' by a fat irritating lesbian who insisted that I felt her swollen mammaries.

'They shouldn't be hard,' she stated emphatically, if a bit drunkenly.

'Well, mine are for looking at, not touching,' I growled back. So much for one big happy Queer community.

I was quite popular with the punters. A creepy Walter Mitty axe-murderer type bought me drinks and said, 'My God – I have a rock-hard erection just sitting beside you.' His arms slid around me with frightening speed. I looked down at his crotch.

Christ – what a fuckwit, I thought, seeing no bulge and anticipating that his ejaculation would be as quick as his arm. So I avoided his bug-eyed stare for the rest of the evening. He cornered me at the end of the night and asked me to go back to Ballygobackwards for a spot of 'mutual fun'. I smiled, smacked his approaching hand and said, 'I'm not that kind of girl. Relationships based on trust and more emotional aspects are what I'm into – not first-night sex!'

'Oh right,' my friend smirked. I wanted to slap his silly face. But that would mean losing at least one nail – more money – and a trip to the poundshop. Scangerville – no! I shuddered at the thought and kept my hand in restraint.

I got home (alone) around three-thirty and crawled into bed after splashing some soap and water over my now disintegrating face. I tossed and turned all night reliving the same recurring dream – or was it a nightmare? – of screwing Joan Collins up against the wall of a cubicle in a men's lavatory. (I must mentions this to my psychiatrist.) Maybe it was my subconscious acting butch in Bruce's absence but I doubt it.

Monday
Arriving at the post office around two o'clock, the usual motley crew were there. Pensioners and oulfellas nursing hangovers, reeking of tobacco and piss. Swishing to the counter I noticed a new cute guy sitting behind the hatch. Black hair, dark eyes and complexion, my favourite. Fluttering my lashes I handed over my dole card. My efforts received a strange look and a measley £61. Disappointed, I continued on to my local Quinnsworth. Again swarming

Tallaght Trash

with pensioners – the fuckers! Everybody passing by seemed to give me a queer look – but not the kind I appreciated. I decided to splash out since a certain hungry bastard was gone for the week. Rushing around the store my list was assimilated in five minutes flat. At the checkout the young scangery girl looked at me incredulously and giggled to her co-worker – a bag-packer (what a career!). Paranoia was descending quickly. What's so strange about a guy buying Oil of Ulay, a facial wash, Vo5 hot-oil treatment, mud mask, body lotion (the non-dancing variety)* and cold cream? No food apart from a lettuce – my perpetual diet regime

After speed-mincing home, the reflection in the mirror gave me the answer to my earlier paranoia. A thick layer of No.7 mascara was still glued to my lashes, above and below! Obviously being bollixed last night didn't help my cleansing routine. I dutifully removed all traces of my make-up and had a mug of steaming hot coffee – my usual breakfast. Swiftly downing a Valium, I realised why I felt so freaked – not taking one the moment I awoke as usual. Life isn't easy for a drag queen, or any sort of queen, especially when you were brought up in Tallaght. (Bring in the violins.) Fab parents but a crap neighbourhood and common-as-muck people. I don't mean to generalise about Hets, but young socio-economically and cerebrally challenged ones are the worst, male or female. At least obnoxious middle-class breeders hurl insults instead of bricks.

Aware that I was having a bad case of Monday-morning(ish) blues/hangover/self-pity (again), I decided to do something positive and life-affirming. Shopping can really cheer a girl up. I share with my sister a passion for shoes that would rival even Imelda Marcos's. So I headed straight for Simon Harts in the Ilac Centre. A sale was underway and they were getting rid of old stock at cheapo

---

* Referring to a now defunct talentless dance troupe which frequented a Dublin nightclub.

prices. Fab, I thought, rifling through a pile of women's shoes and finding a few size eights. At the very bottom was a beautiful five-inch-high platform with peephole toe and slingback in my size – a dream come true. I grabbed it and marched over to the assistant behind the till.

'How much do these cost?' I enunciated, holding it up for inspection.

An expression of surprise struggled with one of disbelief on her face and finally settled into grim disgust. 'About a fiver,' she belched back.

I was shocked that at her age (going by her lines, mid-forties) she hadn't come across any drag queens or even trannies before. After all, it was only a fucking shoe.

'Grand, I'll try it on so.' Sitting down, I eased my delicate foot in. A perfect fit, even with a thick woolly sock on.

The evil cow glared at me as I handed over the cash. 'No exchange or refund under any circumstances,' she blurted in a tone suited to curdling milk. (Maybe it was a little hobby of hers).

'Fine, thank you very much,' I beamed. I strode out of the shop, head held high.

One small step (pardon the pun) for *moi*, one big one for Queerkind.

Tuesday
Brii-ing, brii-ing, brii-ing. The frigging front-door bell went right through my frontal lobe, reverberating endlessly. I staggered downstairs, grabbing a dressing gown on the way.

'Yes?' I bellowed, reefing the door practically off its hinges.

The cute black guy, earlier thirties, stepped back bemused. 'Mr Thompson, Flat four?'

I nodded in the affirmative. I had completely forgotten about the Community Welfare Officer's visit. I had overslept and had the familiar hangover from hell due to sharing a bottle of plonk and some cans with my best friend Peter last night. It was the usual Monday-night heart-to-heart and gossip session.

'See you Thursday when you collect your cheque,' Mr Welfare Officer said, turning and leaving.

Nice bum, I thought. Pity I looked like Michael Jackson without his makeup.

After two disprin, a valium and a coffee, I was human again.

Lunching with my literary agent, we discussed my latest project, *Tallaght Trash*. 'The story of a young girl, Trisha Thompson, who rises above her working-class background to become an internationally renowned supermodel. She is head of her own company and has a PhD in theoretical physics on the side,' I explained. Quantum and sexual mechanics – my two favourite subjects – all in the one nove.

Excitedly, I bounced up and down on the seat, gesticulating wildly. I wanted her to like my ideas, since Bruce doesn't support my literary leanings. Outlining more, I even rashly ordered food. Picking at my diet yoghurt and sipping my black coffee, calorie-counting, I awaited her reply. 'Glitter, glamour, sex, success.'

'*Fabulous*,' she screeched.

'Ab Fab,' I corrected her.

She smiled broadly, stretching her thick lips. Very kosher-looking: doe eyes, large-ish nose, big lips and fluffed brown hair. The only woman who has ever given me an erection. I think this due to my devotion to the wonderful Babs. The sound of 'Evergreen' still sends shudders of satisfaction up and down my spine.

I agreed to have the first chapter drafted in two weeks' time. The rest of the day was spent bouncing ideas around while crocheting myself a hot little number for the weekend.

Wednesday Night
I had an enjoyable night out in the pub with Peter and a few friends. It was the first time I'd been since Bruce and I became an item. But it was a bit disappointing still seeing the same old faces. Jurassic Park seemed to be ever-expanding,

almost taking over the whole place. Leaving early, around one-ish, I trudged home.

Getting to my flat meant walking up a very dimly-lit laneway. Needless to say, it was very cruisy late at night. I always got a tingling anticipation in my bowels going down there – a mixture of sexual hunger and a fear of being bashed senseless by some mad fag-hater. Or maybe it was the dodgy chips I had eaten on the way home. Seeing a male ahead, I flung the remaining chips aside and thought, He's a man, he's got a cock and he's breathing – what the hell. I changed my sashay to a gentle restrained swish and walked towards the guy who was waiting ahead. Passing each other we gave each other a lustful stare, and seeing that it was reciprocated, a smile.

'Follow me,' he whispered. He led both of us across two roads and down a very black alley behind a nearby football ground. His dick was out. I reached down and gave it a squeeze. He was a bit chubby but fat and thick where it counted. When I began to pull him off he removed my hand and unzipped my fly.

'What about you?' I asked.

'I'm fine – just relax and enjoy.'

Starting slowly, he quickly built up his speed and soon I spurted all over his green jacket. Seeing that it was Dunnes Stores and polyester I didn't bother apologising – it would wash out in a jiffy.

Then we introduced ourselves. Later we went back to his des res and had tea. Realising that he was as camp as knickers and had a deeply troubling addiction to Mariah Carey, I left. He pressed, by way of payment I felt, a Kylie CD into my hand. At least it was a good one – 'Rhythm of Love'. I'm not that cheap after all.

Thursday

Amazingly, I managed to make it to the Health Board early. I made a special effort – showered, shaved, a dab of concealer under the eyes and a smattering of translucent powder. The clothes let me down, though. Well, they had to be shabby. John Rocha in a rent-allowance office looks incongruous. My officer, or screw, as I prefer to call him, was particularly nice. The combination of the restricted space, the smell of Escape he was wearing and the flourish with which he signed the cheque really turned me on.

Feeling stupidly happy and randy, gaily swishing along the road, I noticed a car following me. Was I having delusions? No, someone was cruising at ten-thirty in the morning. It was a bit dodgy so I ignored the car and got some groceries in the local shop. When I came out he was still waiting, lights flashing, and giving an occasional beep of the horn. Not being able to control myself, I walked over and opened the passenger door. I brought him home.

After having a fairly enjoyable time, he ruined it all by talking about his weirdo girlfriend. She wanted to watch him fucking another guy dressed in lacy lingerie. I wasn't impressed. He suggested that I could be his little whore. Jesus fucking Christ. I always attract the psychos, I thought, remembering the guy on Sunday. So I fobbed him off with my phone number. I had better things to do than be chased around the room wearing stockings and suspenders. Anyway, my plan for the afternoon was total self-absorption in beauty products and inner contemplation.

Hip to the left – then swing right back again. I practised my walk while Kylie followed by Dusty Springfield followed by Kylie again blasted from the stereo at full volume. I was shimmying around the room waiting for my mud pack to fully harden when the phone rang. It was Peter. All I could manage was 'mmm' to his suggestion of a trip to Cork. I really wanted to scream 'Fab,' but couldn't for fear of severe facial injury. So I swung my foot back and forth to dry the nail varnish and dissipate the excitement I felt thinking of big butch GAA players with thighs of steel. Corkmen always had the best developed ones.

'We could stay at my friend Jim's place,' I suggested

when I called Peter back after my beauty routine. 'He knows all the best cruising places and I hear that the back of Cork bus station is one of the best.'

It was settled then – we were going by Bus Eireann at one o'clock the next afternoon.

Saturday

I caught my breath at the top of the stairs. The ascent was difficult enough and I wanted to compose myself for the grand entrance. It was the first time Linda Vagina-Blister had graced the Cork scene with her presence. I had planned to do in Cork what Debbie had done to Dallas but last night in the pub the only things worth shagging were the bar staff and they were lesbians. It was a sign of desperation – that's why I needed tonight to be an uplifting experience.

Peter and Jim had already entered. 'Fuck it,' I whispered and pushed open the door. Total silence followed and as I slowly pranced across the room the only audible sound was the clunk, clunk, clunk of my platforms on the pine floor. It would have been okay if the club was empty – but it was packed with people gawping and nudging. Well I could hardly slink into the background in what I was wearing – basically a white bra and pants with a woollen crocheted mesh stretched over, very short and laced tightly at the back with cut-outs at the waist. The whole ensemble was completed by a platinum white wig, almost waist-length, and white-tipped eye-lashes.

It was quickly established that the crowd wasn't hostile, just stunned. I was soon introduced by Tom (a friend of Jim's and an absolute ride) to a crowd of very friendly if vertically challenged hairdressers. They followed me around for the whole night, screaming their tits off and screeching, 'You look Fab, girl,' in a shrill Cork accent. I quickly felt Fab and lapped up the adulation. (Ego overkill.)

Tom and I got on like the proverbial house on fire. (Well, he was hot enough to start one.) We discussed Foucault,

Tallaght Trash

Nietzsche, quantum physics and Abba. One the dancefloor I did my usual routine and frightened off a few people. But near the end of the night everyone was up and I was as high as a kite. They lined the walls and watched as I shook, shimmied and sweated to the sometimes v. dated music. ('Vogue'??) At the very end they played a slow set. Tom and I were welded so closely together even a blowtorch couldn't separate us. I also knew that he wasn't Jewish.

Sunday

Tom awoke me from slumber with a kiss full on the lips. The past few hours had been the most sensual ones of my life. Jim had let us sleep on the floor while he and Peter shared a bed. Tom made us all breakfast and later escorted us with Jim to the bus station.

On the way back to Dublin Peter entertained me by telling of the strange gasping noises, slurping and shouts of ecstasy which kept him awake during the night. 'At one stage, I peeped out from under the covers and saw two legs in the air accompanied by a lapping sound. It will haunt me for the rest of my days.'

'Don't be so tight-arsed or you'll suck up the seat,' I replied.

The rest of the trip was spent in silence. I didn't care – I had RuPaul on my Walkman and used the time to mull over my 'relationship' with Bruce.

By the time we reached Busáras my mind was made up. I went home, showered, put on my best make-up and dragged up to the nines: silver hotpants, cropped top, bomber jacket, platforms and a cheeky little silver cap atop a black wig to complete the look. I ordered a black cab – the only one big enough to hold Bruce's Phil Collins collection – and travelled to the airport in style.

When Bruce saw me in the Arrivals Hall he was visibly shaken. He marched over white with rage and shook my shoulders.

'What the fuck is going on? What the bloody hell are you doing dressed like that?'

I removed his hands, composed myself and said, 'Your stuff is in a taxi outside. I've had time to think and I've come to two conclusions: one, you have appalling taste in music, and two, you don't really know how to use what's between your legs properly.'

'You *bitch*,' he yelled.

'Yeah – that's right. I'm a bitch about being my fucking self.'

'Who would have you? What are you going to do now? Hey?' he said.

I turned and walked away. I knew exactly what to do. Tom's number was in my bag and I was going to give him a call.